Jacob Kerr was born in 1... rural Northumberland. This...

Praise for *The Green Man of Eshwood Hall*

'This evocative short novel is a work of folk horror, close in spirit to Alan Garner's fantasies rooted in the land' *Guardian*

'Skilfully evokes a nation, its old certainties overturned by war, on the cusp of social upheaval and change' *Financial Times*

'A novel about vanity, selfishness and exploitation . . . beautifully written and heart-breaking' *Literary Review*

'One of those books that enchant you to the point of distraction; so engrossing, you crave more precious reading time. It offers the reader a classic adventure story, delivers ample scares and supernatural peril, and shows that for all her real-world woes, the protagonist's life can still get infinitely worse. An absolute treasure of a novel, one that reminds you what a joy reading can be' *Buzz Magazine*

'Kerr's eco-horror preaches embracing rather than avoiding your fears. A terrifying prospect indeed' *Irish Times*

'Kerr, a rare talent, has created something unique. A multi-genre piece, it draws on folk tales and stories of servants and masters to create something unlike anything the reader has read before . . . Truly unputdownable' *Bookmunch*

The Green Man of Eshwood Hall

A Tale of Northalbion

Jacob Kerr

This paperback edition first published in 2023
First published in Great Britain in 2022 by
Serpent's Tail,
an imprint of Profile Books Ltd
29 Cloth Fair
London
ECIA 7JQ
www.serpentstail.com

Copyright © Jacob Kerr, 2022

Text design by Crow Books

1 3 5 7 9 10 8 6 4 2

'Chicken Road' words and music (p.16–17) by Joe Greene © 1954 (Renewed)
FRANK MUSIC CORP.
All rights reserved.
Reprinted by permission of Hal Leonard Europe Ltd.

Printed and bound in Great Britain by
CPI Group (UK) Ltd, Croydon CR0 4YY

A CIP catalogue record for this book is available from the British Library.

ISBN 978 1 80081 1515

eISBN 978 1 80081 1508

for Helen

If I could choose
Freely in that great treasure-house
Anything from any shelf,
I would give you back yourself . . .

Edward Thomas, 'And You, Helen'

Contents

Prologue

1962

This is the story of a girl called Isabella; but no one ever called her Isabella: they called her Izzy. She didn't like being called Izzy but didn't suppose there was much she could do about it – she was only thirteen and small for her age. It was an embarrassing name because it rhymed with 'frizzy' and 'dizzy', and when Mrs Hartop said one of these words (and Mrs Hartop, of course, had such a loud voice!) then Izzy would jump in her seat because she'd hear the sound of her name and think she was going to get wrong. Once, Mrs Hartop had told the class that they should be hard at work, and that they should be 'Busy, busy, busy!' and Izzy felt her face go bright red. It was silly, really, because Izzy was a good girl and stayed very quiet and hardly ever got wrong for anything. And anyway, she didn't go to school at all any more because she had to look after Mam.

This is also the story of Izzy's mother, Geraldine. Not

that she let anyone call her that. You had to call her Gerry. What her parents were thinking when they decided to burden her with a name like Geraldine she'd never know. To be perfectly frank, she didn't like 'Gerry' much either, but it would have to do.

Izzy had a younger sister called Annie, who was eight and wanted a horse, and a baby brother, whose name was Raymond, but, because he was the youngest, everyone just called him the Bairn. He'd been named after his father, who will also be in the story.

Most of all, though, this is the story of the Green Man of Eshwood Hall, whose name, supposing that he had a name, nobody ever learned – not even Izzy, and she came to know him better than anyone.

I

Eshwood Hall

I

The Whipper family's Humber Hawk, luggage tied to its roof, wobbled on its jammy springs up the poplar-lined driveway towards Eshwood Hall. It was a March morning, and the first day of spring according to the almanacs, but this was the North where the winters don't let go easily: patches of stubborn snow clung to the verges. The snowdrops were out but little else. The Whippers saw glimpses of the River Esh, now far off in the grassy bends between trees, now snaking close by the car. All around them was Eshwood Forest, and deep within Eshwood Forest stood the Chapel, though the Whippers weren't to know this yet. Every now and then a robin flicked to a hedge-top to take a look at them approaching, and then flicked away again.

The Humber Hawk had been bought new five years ago, and had in that time been subjected to various improvements at the hands of its owner, Ray: if you were to look under the bonnet, you would see that the Hawk had the components of a number of other makes of car in addition to its own. Next to Ray, who was driving of course, sat Gerry. Gerry didn't drive and didn't work because of her weak heart. She was holding the Bairn close to her breast, as though she expected to be greeted by someone who might try to take him away from her. The lasses were in the back of the car. Annie stared through one window and then another, as excited as her dad. Izzy spent her time watching her parents, trying to gauge the mood.

They had passed the abandoned lodge house at the gateposts, and now they passed the rose garden, sun-dappled and deserted, and now, rounding a corner, they were met with the great blank stare of Eshwood Hall. At the last crunch of the gravel, a hush fell over the Humber Hawk like a veil; no sound but the distant murmurings of the River Esh and the wind in the trees.

The Whippers looked up at the Hall that loomed before them: fluted columns; corbie-stepped gable; rusticated quoins and pilasters ... Izzy would have described it as 'ancient' – a word she liked – but in fact it had stood for less than two centuries, built on its three-hundred-acre site in 1776 by a mine-owner named Wallis whose pretensions had led him to reinvent himself as a banker; by this means it had taken him a little under forty years to lose his riches, whereupon he sold the Hall and land to John Brooks, an ironmaster from Oldshield. Brooks had held on to it for half that time before it bankrupted him. In fact, although the Whippers would not learn this until much later, the Hall had brought nothing but bad luck to each of its owners as it passed to and fro between the newest of the new wealth and the last of the old. Presently it was owned by the Claiborne family, old Colonel Claiborne having washed up there after fleeing Glendale Hall in Co. Wexford during the rising – the rebellion, as he'd have put it. The Claiborne family now consisted of one aged spinster (the Colonel's only surviving daughter) and a fleet of interested second cousins. Ashlared, green-slated, seven-bayed, the Hall must have been grand in its day, but now, swaddled in ivy, it was slipping back into its preferred state of disrepair, and even Izzy could see that her dad was going to have his work cut out for him.

Annie leapt from the car straight onto her imaginary horse and trotted towards the steps that led up to the main entrance. 'Is this really where we're going to live?'

Ray got out of the car and stretched his stiff limbs in the chilly sunshine. He pulled on his cap. 'This is the Hall all right. Very canny, eh? Fancy, eh? Didn't I tell you? Now, do you want to see your room? What about you, Izzy, do you want to see your room?'

Izzy took this as permission to leave the car. Gerry climbed out warily, holding the Bairn close. She regarded the north wing of the Hall where the servants' quarters were; its wonky roof and unwashed windows – obviously the part where the skivvies were kept. Home, sweet home! The roof was the real worry, though. Gerry, indulging her habit of finding fault, had spotted the missing tiles when they were driving up to the place.

Ray, following her gaze, said, 'We'll get that fixed up soon enough, no bother . . .'

And then Ray was guiding Annie's imaginary horse away

from the main entrance and towards the more modest door that they would use, down at the far end of the north wing, with Gerry hurrying after them, still carrying the Bairn. Izzy, unexpectedly left alone, looked around and felt the reality of the move break over her in a wave. They moved house every year or so, following whatever work Dad could find, and then upping sticks when Mam couldn't take it any more. Izzy had never known it to be any other way, and moving around wasn't so bad, apart from having to change schools all the time, though of course that was all done with now that she had to look after Mam full-time. Still, this move felt different, more daunting. They'd be living in the biggest house she'd ever seen.

Izzy stepped back and considered Eshwood Hall, and, for all she knew, it considered her. To a child, which is what Izzy was, after all, an imposing old house always has an air of excitement mixed with sadness, and so this one had for Izzy. Likewise, children always see faces and attitudes in houses, and so Izzy did in the sullen facade before her: Eshwood Hall, she thought, was shrugging its wings, hunching its shoulders, raising its palms to heaven. *I'd like to, but I can't*, it seemed to say. She pushed some gravel around with the toe of her shoe. There were weeds sprouting up here and there all along the driveway – once you'd noticed them, you saw them everywhere, little signs of neglect. She looked up at an oak tree, and then up, higher, through the branches that swayed gently in the river of wind, then up again into the pale sky . . . The cold had crept through her clothes already; her face was numb.

Annie threw open one of the second-floor windows and stuck her head out: 'I've already picked which bed's mine. My coat's on it now so I've got dibs.'

Ray appeared in the window beside Annie, tugging her back inside playfully. 'It's all right, Izzy, you've got the window bed anyway.'

Izzy felt another wave breaking over her: they didn't have rooms of their own. She made her way into the Hall and up the stairs to confirm this.

Ray caught her look of disappointment and, because he had already decided that he liked the place and wanted everyone else to like it too, he said, 'Sorry, pet. But it's a big room. Annie'll drop down between the floorboards. You'll hardly notice her.'

But the room *wasn't* big. People shouldn't be allowed to say a room was big when it wasn't. There were two small beds, and Annie was lying determinedly on one, trying to make herself as heavy as possible in case Izzy tried to turf her off. Izzy went to the next room – that would be her parents'; there was a double bed in there and Mam was sitting on it, nursing the Bairn and watching Izzy steadily. Izzy turned away and opened the last door. This room was tiny, with one very small window through which the sky was just visible.

Izzy returned to her room and sat down gently next to Annie. She asked Annie if she'd seen the little extra room. Annie nodded cautiously. Izzy said that she thought that was the best room in the place, because it was so small it was hidden and secret.

'Why don't you ask for it to be your room, then?' asked Annie.

Izzy said that she could, but she had thought Annie might like it for herself, and as she'd had first dibs on the bed, it was only fair for her to have first dibs on the room. But Annie wasn't that daft, and said Izzy was just trying to get her to take the little room so she, Izzy, could have the big room to herself. This had, in fact, been Izzy's wish. She changed tack.

'Ok, *I'll* have the little room. I'd rather have the little room. I think it's excellent. But you should ask Mam and Dad if I can have it: you know they'll say no if I ask.'

Annie saw at once the deep injustice in being asked to do something she didn't have to do. 'Why should *I* ask them? If you want the room, *you* should ask.'

'Because if *I* ask they'll say *no* like always, and then we'll have to share this room. But if you ask *for* me, they might say *yes*, and then you can have this room to yourself, you see?'

Annie thought about this for some moments.

'And anyway, Dad *promised* us that we'd have our own rooms this time, so it's only fair.'

Annie clambered from the bed and trotted through to her parents' bedroom. Izzy listened as the request was made . . . and struck down at once, as Gerry said that the little room was to be the Bairn's room.

'But he doesn't *need* his own room. He's always with you!' Annie improvised.

'He's your *brother*,' Gerry reminded her.

'Dad said we could have our *own* rooms this time. He *promised*. I don't *want* to share with Izzy!'

'Ray, you didn't . . .?'

'I said I'd do my best to make sure you got your own rooms. Look, we're not even moved in yet. There'll be something I can do.' Ray could feel the peace unravelling already. He reflected, not for the first time, that there was little point in trying to keep things on an even keel, with three women in the house and all of them impossible.

Gerry, who could see where this was going, put an end to it by telling Annie that she'd be sharing a bedroom with her sister and that was that.

With a last accusing glance at Ray, Annie pushed out of the box room and ran back in to see Izzy. She shrugged; Izzy nodded. It had been a long shot.

Izzy lay on her bed, gazing out of the window, aware of her mother's voice following Ray as he pottered from their bedroom down to the parlour-kitchen, pointing out that he was forever making promises he couldn't keep, and that he'd be making the Bairn a cot before he started clarting on dividing up rooms. The parlour? He wasn't doing anything to the parlour. He was going to get the electric working first of all, that's what he was going to do. Jesus Christ. A Hall this size and she gives us three and a half poky little rooms. She must be all heart.

*

And so, as the hours creep by, the Whippers move in. Picture them carrying boxes and dragging bags from the car into

9

the Hall – from the servants' entrance, making their way up an old-fashioned oak staircase (their rooms being on the first and second floors), and joining a long dim passage, at one end of which lay the great door which communicated with the rest of the Hall. On one of their first trips from the car to their apartments, Ray tells Izzy and Annie in no uncertain terms that they were not to go playing in the Hall beyond this point, and if they did ever have to go through that door for any reason, they would need to be on best behaviour, else they'd get a hiding. Here's Ray carrying armfuls of bedding upstairs; there's Izzy in the parlour, raking out the clinker and ash from the fire and polishing the metalwork with black lead; and even little Annie is helping, sweeping out the bedrooms.

Gerry is arranging her collection of china figurines on the Welsh dresser. Gerry has almost twenty figurines, mostly women in various approximations of the fashions of the last century; some are mothers with babies in their arms, but most of them are young women doing nothing but pose wistfully, gazing with a mysterious smile into the middle distance, perhaps waiting for a gentleman caller who will never come since Gerry doesn't own any male figurines. All of the figures are made of white china with details picked out in a slightly faded royal blue glaze. Having no toys of her own, Izzy has made a careful and secret comparison of them, and she knows their every detail and tiniest flaw. They are, she supposes, very expensive. They are certainly the most expensive thing the family owns, after the car, and maybe Dad's record player. And now Gerry – who, it need hardly be added, has strictly forbidden her children to touch her figurines – has finished arranging them, with the mothers holding babies given pride of place at the front, for she has her favourites, even among these.

2

From the kitchen window Izzy watched her dad moving boxes of tools and other apparatus from the car into his work-shed, which was just visible at the far end of the north wing. Dad was a friendly sort. Mam said he was too friendly and 'givish', which meant he was the opposite of selfish but just as bad. Izzy saw him hail a man who was weeding. This man, the gardener presumably, jabbed his hoe into the earth and ambled over to Ray. The gardener was just shy of fifty years old, and though he wasn't quite as tall as Ray, he was much stockier, all neck and shoulders. Ray looked even more slender and less real by comparison. Together the two men unstrapped the last and biggest piece of luggage, a long wooden crate, from the roof of the car and lifted it down carefully. Annie popped up beside Izzy at the window. On tiptoe she could just see out.

'Who's that?'

Izzy didn't see how she could be expected to know this, and said so.

'He looks dirty. I bet he smells. You smell.'

'I think he's the gardener. I think he's been digging,' said Izzy, not unreasonably.

'What's he been digging?'

Izzy didn't see how she could be expected to know this, either.

'Dirty potatoes!' shouted Annie, and squealed with laughter at her joke. They both watched Ray and the gardener carry the crate into the long, rickety shed that stood adjacent to the Hall, where they disappeared out of sight.

'Where are they taking it?'

Knowing that there would be no end to Annie's questions if she was in the mood, Izzy volunteered to go and find out, and report back afterwards.

The shed would be Ray's workshop, his centre of operations; if anyone wanted him, this would be the first place they'd look. Its doors stood open, and seemed as if they had been standing open for so long they had put down roots. Izzy could hear her father's voice from inside: 'That's it, that's it, just set that end down. Now, if I just pivot – oh, nearly! Hold on, hold on – I've got to get this end over here. You steady it for me – that's it – perfect – no!' There was a crash, as something fell over and knocked something else over. 'It didn't catch you, did it? Thank goodness. No, I'm right as rain, just . . . You'll be wondering what's in here, won't you? Well, not today, but one of these days, once we're all unpacked, I'll give you the tour . . .'

Izzy had noticed this about her father, that he could talk for two when necessary. She had also noticed that few grown-ups seemed interested in his inventions, which was puzzling when you considered how many of them there were, and how amazing it was going to be when one of them worked. Now he was telling the gardener about the modifications he'd made to their car.

'The Macpherson struts rusted, obviously, so I welded those. And I swapped the engine with one from a Sceptre. It's an overdrive, so when you let your foot off the throttle, it doesn't slow down, it just cruises along, because the balls only slowly fall out of the cone, so it doesn't have the retardation of an ordinary gearbox, you see? It all works by pressure, which is created by the pump in front of the overdrive, and once that's engaged by the electrical coil, the lever opens a valve that transfers the pressure that's built up to the pistons that engage the cone clutch, creating the overdrive position. Proper bastard to start, though but.'

Now she'd heard Dad say a rude word, so she'd get wrong if he caught her listening . . . She looked through the gap between the doors and saw the gardener looking without much interest at the paraphernalia already collected in the shed. Now Dad was talking about energy, and how it was all around us all the time, and how once we'd found a way to capture it, no one would have to work any more. This was one of his favourite things to talk about. He was pointing at something on his latest project: 'Now, when the oscillators are connected in the circuit the condensers only slowly fill up – they don't take the charge right off, you see? And the longer the current charges them the more charge they'll take. And these lights are red hot, what with the incandescence of the gas in the globes here, under the VHF. And this is the interesting thing: if it was an ordinary current, the size of wire in the transformer would never carry the amperage passing through it: it would burn to a frazzle – but here the wires stay perfectly cool and it doesn't matter how long the machine's been running. Now, isn't that interesting?'

Izzy stepped out into the sunlight again, and ran back to the Hall. On her way up the stairs she startled a short, large-bosomed woman who wore a funny sort of bonnet that looked too small for her head, and which had the effect of making the rest of her body seem even more stout and solid. The woman clutched her side, pretending to be startled, and asked who Izzy was.

'I'm Izzy. Isabella.'

'Make your mind up.'

'Izzy.'

'Izzy. Right. You must be Izzy Whipper. I'm Sheila. You var-nigh knocked us over! Now, then. Where's your mam and dad?'

Ray appeared at the foot of the stairs before Izzy could answer. 'Here, I'm here: Raymond Whipper . . .'

'So you made it all right?' said Sheila.

'Oh, aye, very well, thank you. Just getting our things unloaded and that . . .'

Sheila introduced herself as the Chief Cook, and named some of the other staff that the Whippers would meet in due course: Wilkes, the footman, and Mr Henderson, the keeper, and so forth. Sheila lived in the rooms next door to the Whippers, with her husband, Bob, and her daughter, Biddy. Then she broke the news: 'Miss Claiborne was expecting you to call on her this morning.'

Ray, seeing that he'd made an error on his first day, and a bad first impression, looked stricken, and offered to go up to see her there and then.

'No, she's no good in the afternoons – best leave it till the morn. The doctor's out then, though, so I don't know . . . I'll tell her you're here. You're best off just waiting to be called.'

'Is there something I should be getting on with in the meantime?'

Sheila laughed. 'I don't know, *is* there?'

'I'll have a look around.'

She fixed him with a slow, flat gaze, before taking pity on him: 'You might make a start in the kitchen. The flue's stenshin'. Dead bird, no doubt.'

At this, Ray looked relieved, and thanked Sheila heartily. He really was a friendly sort.

3

The electric was down throughout the north wing, so that evening Ray rigged an extension cable through the window which meant he could power up his Pye Black Box, his most treasured possession. A house without music could never feel like home. He selected a favourite 78 of 'Tennessee' Ernie Ford, and soon while Izzy prepared the meal she could hear the familiar strains of 'Chicken Road' uncoiling through the parlour:

Once I got a splinter
In the joint of my little toe
And a garter snake bit my knee
By the bend of the little St. Joe.
Honey, that's misery . . .

When Gerry and Ray had started courting, the Victory Day bunting had still been up on the Town Hall. Ray had once said – he'd had a drink on him at the time, yes, but still, he'd meant it seriously enough – that people should just leave the bunting up permanently, and never stop celebrating victory. Why not? Who decided when a victory was over? People needed something to keep their spirits up, what with rationing and strikes and what-have-you. In time, of course, the bunting had come down, but by moving around so much, fresh start after fresh start, the Whippers had preserved something of that sense of make-do and merry befuddlement that everyone seemed to feel back then. Gerry and Ray could still be childlike. They could be childish. They took no interest in things that didn't interest them, which is a habit more usual in folk wealthier than they. Back in the day, they had liked doing new things – going to the pictures, dancing, or going to a show – and nowadays they liked getting new things, like the telly, which they'd had to sell in the end so they could afford the record player.

While Izzy prepared their tea at the range, Gerry nursed the Bairn. Annie was keeping quiet for once, concentrating on her crayons. For their first proper meal in their new home, Izzy was making tinned salmon rissoles followed by marmalade pudding. On account of her mother's heart condition, Izzy took care of almost all of the cooking for the family. It was Izzy who, each morning after she'd fetched the coal from the bunker, made the pot of porridge, or boiled the eggs, or fried the bacon and tomatoes for breakfast; and for tea she could make cheese and potato flan, or spam fritters, or leek pudding, or panacalty, which was bacon and potatoes plus cheese and whatever else was there to be had. And then, for afters, they might have stewed fruit, or, if there had been time for to make it, bread and butter pudding, or something like that. At bedtime, it was Izzy who, after she'd done the dishes, made the cocoa and filled the hot-water bottles for Annie and Gerry, before she banked the fire with slack last thing.

> Once I had a scorpion
> On the lobe of my good right ear
> And a great-great grandma
> Who could hear what she wanted to hear.
> Honey, that's misery . . .

'Hey there, *honey*,' intoned Ray from the other room, imitating Ford's bass-baritone, 'you know he isn't saying "that's *misery*", he's saying "that's *Missouri*". Mih-*zoo*-ree. It's a place in America, like.'

Izzy, who hadn't realised that she'd been singing along, blushed furiously.

Without taking her eyes off the Bairn, Gerry said, 'Nitwit.'

The potatoes were coming to the boil, juggling against the saucepan lid and making it tremble and chatter. That was good. Izzy had been worried the range wouldn't be hot enough.

'Ray,' said Gerry, 'that Sheila . . . what's her story, do you reckon?'

'Oh, I hardly know . . .' said Ray, getting up, though he'd only just sat down, to go and leaf through his 78s again. Not that he'd have admitted it, but Gerry's tone had made him jumpy. It was the tone she used when she was looking for a problem. Ray was as sensitive as an elliptical stylus to Gerry's tone. All he wanted was a nice evening relaxing after a long drive. Maybe he should have put on Johnny Cash instead. He held up an LP: 'Hey, do you remember when we got this . . .?'

Bubbles and starchy foam were breaking out from the sides of the lid as the potatoes jostled in the pan. It was a good boil, but it just kept building.

'I mean, she took her sweet time coming around here, didn't she? And then she's one word to you, and that's it, she's off. That's not what I'd call a welcome. I can't say I felt welcomed at all.'

Water splashed over the side of the pan onto the hotplate, where it hissed and scattered a mad panic of dancing drops, the pan-lid chattering like crazy, foam bulging and bursting from the rim.

'Jesus Christ!' Gerry cried.

'The hotplate's too hot . . .'

'Well, turn it down, then!'

But Gerry knew that there was no way to turn it down. The hotplates were heated by the fire, which couldn't be stoked or cooled very rapidly at all. Izzy took the lid off the pan to let the steam out, and up it flew in a great white plume that closed around her wrist. She dropped the lid with a crash as she gasped with the shock and the pain.

'For Christ's sake!'

'Izzy, pet, you can't startle your mam like that . . .'

The Bairn, who had woken when Gerry jumped, began to cry, his high wail mixing uneasily with 'Tennessee' Ernie Ford's rumbling voice. But the job was done: the water rolled but didn't rise, the potatoes bustled happily. Izzy flashed her wrist under the tap.

'There, there,' Gerry said, jiggling the Bairn on her lap. To Izzy she said, 'You've not got the brains you were born with, I swear. They fell out when the midwife slapped your arse.' She had said this many times before; Izzy paid it no mind. 'And when will this triumph be ready?'

'I'm *starving*,' Annie said.

'We're all starving. After the day we've had, carting all our goods and chattels about, and then not even a glass of water offered us when we arrived. That Sheila could've spared us a bite from the kitchen, couldn't she? Not even a sandwich! Please, Lady Muck, spare us an HP Sauce sandwich, for pity's sake!'

'I had a bit something,' Ray said, 'when I was there . . .'

'Oh, yes, and what did you have?' Gerry held the still-crying Bairn out to Ray, who hastily put down the record he was holding.

Izzy buttered the sliced bread and slathered some marmalade on top, then broke an egg into a bowl of milk, trying not to include any shell, mixed it up and poured it over the bread. This went in the oven and would be ready in forty-five minutes. The potatoes were waterlogged now. When she drained them in the colander they looked half-mashed already. She opened two tins of salmon and scraped the grey-pink chunks into a bowl with the potatoes and worked it all together with a fork. So much for shaping them into rissoles. When she dropped wet spoonfuls into the hot lard in the frying pan, they spread and merged together to form one huge fritter that sizzled and spat. She flipped it once, and then hacked it into quarters with the wooden spoon.

The Bairn was stopping crying: he gulped a few choppy breaths, and then his face cleared, and all was well once more. Ray was about to hand him back to Gerry when Izzy called that their tea was ready, so the Bairn was put down in his cot and the rest of the family sat down to eat. Their plates were so close on the drop-leaf table they were almost touching.

Gerry said to Izzy, 'You'll give your dad a bit of yours – and Annie will too if she doesn't eat up.' Izzy shovelled some of the rissole-fritter off her plate and onto Ray's. Ray stole a look at Gerry, half-wondering if he'd done something to annoy her.

There were tinned mushy peas on the side, and tea to drink. They poked and chewed in silence for a minute or two, listening to the music and the crackle of the fire, until

Gerry said, 'Well, you'll not be running Sheila out of a job, that's for sure.'

'Don't be too hard on her,' Ray said, and then, 'I could use this for grouting the chimbley!'

'Can I wait for pudding?' Annie asked.

But the pudding, when it emerged, was blackened across the top: the oven had obviously been hotter than Izzy had realised. She chipped the burned layer off and tipped it into the bin, but there remained a faintly smoky taste in the milksoppy bread underneath.

'Well, this is *champion*, as your father would say, isn't it . . .' said Gerry, picking up her spoon then setting it back down in the bowl. 'I'll bet a finer banquet was never had at Eshwood Hall. Wouldn't you say so, Ray? Don't you think we're spoiled?'

Just then, the Bairn started to cry again.

4

That night, Izzy lay in her bed by the window. The moon was full, and she could see a fine mizzle falling on the thousand spires of Eshwood Forest, threatening to turn into snow. The room was uncurtained, and the moonlight fell upon her possessions arranged on the windowsill – her books and her hairbrush – and on her alert face as she gazed up and out at the void. It was her first night in Eshwood Hall, and tired as she was it seemed impossible to sleep.

Annie, in her bed, was also still awake, and found her mind returning to its favourite topic. 'Do you reckon they've got any horses here?'

'Don't reckon they've got much of owt.'

'What do you mean?'

'I mean the place is falling to bits.'

Annie thought on this for a spell. 'You've got to have horses when you live in the country. It's the *law*.'

'What law?'

'The law of the *land*.'

Next door, Gerry was sitting up in bed. Ray was taking an absolute age to get ready. If he kept faffing about, the Bairn, who was asleep at her side, would wake up, and then who would have to get him back to sleep? Not Ray! Gerry would be very upset if that happened. In fact, she could feel herself getting a bit upset at the prospect of this happening. And another thing: 'You didn't introduce me to anyone today. How am I meant to meet anyone round here?'

'There's time for that, pet. We're here now. You'll be sick of them afore long. You'll meet everyone soon, and we'll get into the village and all. Maybe not tomorrow, though but. Kitchen flue's in a right state.'

'There's a surprise . . .'

Ray finally got into bed. Gerry looked slightly annoyed to have him there with her. Ray reached out tentatively towards his wife and touched her sternum gently. 'How's my pretty ticker?'

'Just the same.' That was what Gerry always said when

someone asked her how she was doing or how she was feeling or how things were. 'Just the same,' she'd say. She had a fond hope that some day they might take the hint. That was the worst thing about being ill: people were constantly asking how you were, hoping you'd say that you were feeling better so that *they* could feel better. So she made a point of always telling them she felt just the same. Unless, of course, she felt worse.

'You need sleep. You're tired out. Lie down properly, pet. Lie down . . .'

Ray was soon asleep. He fell asleep as easily as a child, letting go of whatever cares he had. In the morning he'd wake up just as quickly, and be up and off, whistling something or other, for he'd ever a tune in his head. Gerry sat in the bed, drowsing with open eyes. Her nerves were jangled from the long drive, and when she closed her eyes she felt like she was still hurtling down the road in that bloody car. It was like being tipsy, except she hadn't had the pleasure of a drink. Eventually, thinking such thoughts as these, she drifted into sleep.

In the girls' room, Izzy was the only one left awake. The moon had moved away from the window and the room was darker now. In the gloom, the encircling forest seemed to have pushed up closer to the Hall, and the gardens and the driveway looked like frivolous gestures made against the encroaching shadows of the trees. The wind moaned cheerlessly. Izzy imagined the moon sailing in the sky, shining bright over Eshwood Forest, and wondered if there were deer in the woods. To see a roe in the moonlight would be a grand thing. Surely there must be deer out there, and other shy beasts – foxes and otters and red squirrels and pine martens even – but would she get to see any? It was pleasant to think of walking in the woods at night, the cypresses blue in the moonlight, the birches showing white as bone, all other colours lost in the vast purple and black skirts of the mother forest – it was pleasant to think of, but it was spooky as well.

These musings were interrupted by a distant scratching sound, so gentle at first that Izzy had been listening to it for some time before she became aware of it. It was a swirly, scratchy sort of a sound like something being hollowed out, like a curved knife carving and scooping out a soft, fibrous piece of wood. Izzy knew that old houses could make creaks and groans as they settled, especially at night after the fire was out and the stone and the wood were cooling, but she had never heard anything like this before. Queer how she couldn't tell whether the sound was inside or outside her ear, the sort of uncertainty that would keep anyone awake; it had to be close, somewhere in the house, anyway, because its arrival had made the sound of the distant faint rush of the Esh disappear altogether. There it was again – a little louder, or a little nearer, and this time it was a more describable, horrible, intimate sound; it was testing and picking, like someone peeling a potato an inch from her ear. Izzy threw herself down in the bed and pulled the covers tight about her head, but it was no good, she could hear the noise even there.

Suddenly, she recognised it: it wasn't possible, but

she recognised it. It was the sound of Dad's Black Box, endlessly playing the dead wax on a 78, but at full volume and, apparently, from inside her bedroom. To judge by its sound, it must be at her bedside; but, once she had steeled herself to poke her head out from under the covers and take a look, there was nothing there to be seen. There was nothing amiss in the room at all. And then the air burst to life with Ernie Ford's long-drawn bass-baritone. Izzy gasped with fright, jumping rigid in the bed like a bolt slammed in a lock.

> Once I . . . got a sunburn . . .
> On the back of my . . . itchin' neck . . .
> Took a ride with a girl in a Model-T . . .
> And died . . . in a wonderful wreck!

And then, with an ear-splitting rake of noise, the stylus swept across the 78 – and finally, mercifully, silence flooded back into the room. Izzy was holding the covers over her mouth with her fists. Her throat had all but closed in fright. At length, she managed to look over at Annie's bed. Incredibly, Annie had slept through it all. There she lay: eyes closed, mouth open, face blank as a turnip. How had it been possible for her – for anyone – to sleep through such a racket? Why wasn't the Bairn awake, and wailing at the top of his lungs? Why weren't Mam and Dad up and running about? She could hear Dad snoring even now . . .

Although she didn't think she would sleep at all that night, what with her nerves thrilling in the cavernous aftermath of the noise, and nothing for company but the mice and the moon, she supposed she must have drifted off at some point before dawn rolled around.

2

The Grey Lady

I

As with most country houses, much of the history of
Eshwood Hall was written clearly on its walls: it had arisen,
the visitor would infer, by a single-minded effort at the will
of its founder and architect, in order to preserve an idea
of life that could not have existed in actuality without such
a house to embody it. In one particular, however, it was
enigmatical: it faced east. The idea of it doing so by design
baffled the imagination. How could anyone have seen fit
to build a place that kept its back to the rain blowing in
from Ireland? Had it faced west, then you would have seen
the day coming, and been able to take due precautions. As
things were, you took your chances, and often as not found
yourself drenched in a freak shower of rain or caught in
a fall of unseasonable snow from a sky you hadn't seen
goldening.

The uses to which Eshwood Hall had been put since its conception were straightforwardly those its walls implied, except that it had twice in its history been distinguished by use as a military hospital, most recently as a convalescence home for wounded soldiers in the Second World War, and prior to that it had served as a psychiatric clinic for victims of shell shock during the Great War, when it was run by Dr Erasmus Wintergreen.

Wintergreen's fame, or notoriety, as a weird-finder and (when necessary) charlatan-exposer, has tended to over-shadow his first career in psychoanalysis, and it is often forgotten that he was, between 1888 and 1893, an assistant physician at the Burghölzli Hospital in Zurich, specialising in cases of double consciousness and twilight states. This, of course, provided him with a unique angle of approach when it came to spookery, but it also formed the foundation for the groundbreaking new therapies he developed at Eshwood Hall in 1917, including the renowned adaptation of the isolation chamber that he called the Music of the Spheres.

Dr Wintergreen had been known to Colonel Claiborne as early as 1898, when the Colonel called on his services in the aftermath of a family tragedy that necessitated the laying of no fewer than seven ghosts: the spirits, as was immediately understood by all who cared to consider it for a moment, of the seven Claiborne children who had died in infancy. It has been said that a noble family is likely to be proud of having a ghost, and that a haunted room may be worth as much to their vanity as a small farm; but the Claibornes were not exactly noble, and if one ghost was a curio, seven was an infestation. In any case, Dr Wintergreen settled the matter, and the family were untroubled by ghosts thereafter, though rumours persisted as rumours will.

For reasons that have never been satisfactorily explained, the Colonel's return to Eshwood Hall in 1920 seems to have been quickly followed by a falling-out between the two men, and the 'Wintergreen Clinic', as it was informally known, closed its doors shortly thereafter. By 1962, the only sign that it had ever existed were the volumes of Dr Wintergreen's casebook notes neatly filed in the library, and a sundial encrusted with astrological elaborations that the doctor had installed in the south garden, and which now languished in the cellar, its sidereal purposes, if indeed it had any, now long forgotten.

2

Miss Claiborne liked to think – and, even more, she liked to say – that she didn't often stand on ceremony, but one exception that she proudly admitted was when it came to the subject of bread. Shop loaves were absolutely forbidden at Eshwood Hall: Miss Claiborne disliked their taste, smell and texture, and had a vaguer but more rooted objection to the idea of their existence. In consequence, making bread was one of Sheila's weekly tasks. Miss Claiborne had grudgingly accepted Sheila's refusal to do this more than once a week, on the grounds that it was too much faff, and it was agreed that, as was traditional, Thursday would be baking day.

Now, as arranged, Sheila had kept the leftover dough in an old biscuit tin for Izzy to make into stotties. Izzy was up early to get the fire built and the oven warmed. In addition to the stotties, she was going to make a rice pudding. Everything was still new and it would no doubt take her a while to adjust her timings, but the baking seemed to go better than last night's dinner had.

While she worked, Izzy thought of how people would have been baking bread in much the same way in Eshwood Hall for centuries (she was still uncertain about the age of the building), and that made her feel part of a long line of cooks, or bakers, or scullery maids, or what-have-yous (she was also uncertain about the staff who would have worked at the Hall). Candlelight did that, too, she always thought: the way things looked by the candlelight was the way they'd have looked five hundred years ago. The gas lamps, which lit their wing of the Hall, didn't carry you quite so far back, but they were definitely old-fashioned, and Izzy liked the way they never stopped muttering and putt-putting, sipping up air and spitting out tiny flames.

Once the stotties were out and cooling, Izzy went to find Annie and the pair of them spent the rest of the morning exploring the grounds. At that moment the flower beds at the front of the Hall were desolate, and there was nothing to see but shrubs and stumps that had been pruned so severely for winter they still seemed to be in shock. The girls speculated as to the colour of the flowers that would, they hoped, soon grow there. The only flowers Annie could name were daffs and roses. Izzy had tried to teach her the names of wild flowers, or 'simples' as Ray called them – eyebright, fleabane, yellow tormentil – but the names never seemed to take and Annie would soon revert to calling all flowers daffs or roses indifferently. Eventually, to Annie's soon-extinguished delight, they found their way to an area that a sign proclaimed was the rose garden, but the bushes in it seemed as far from life as could be, the dry thorns painful to look at. And there were weeds and bare earth, and most of the grass looked more like some sort of hillocky moss than grass, and always, at the edge of the lawns, the woods. The girls stopped from time to time and looked into the trees, but when Izzy proposed a walk in the woods, Annie cried out that they weren't allowed, and threatened to tell.

'You've got nowt to tell, you chicken, I was only asking,' Izzy muttered. Annie was no fun, always wanting to be off aimlessly gallivanting when they weren't allowed, but at the same time unwilling to bend a rule when to do so might mean an actual bit of adventure.

The row that was surely brewing was luckily avoided when the girls spotted the gardener at work across the way, planting seeds. He didn't have anyone to talk to, so they decided to go over to say hello.

'What kind of flowers you planting?' Annie asked him.

The gardener didn't look up from his work. 'No flowers . . .' he said, but it sounded more like 'nay flooers': his accent was even stronger than Sheila's, and his voice was so deep it seemed to come up from his boots. The girls stole a glance at one another, tempted to laugh, but wary enough of this imposing stranger to hold it back.

'What you planting then?'

When the gardener straightened up he was taller and broader than the girls had realised. He looked blankly at Annie. 'You'll have to wait and see, won't you?'

'How long'll we have to wait?'

'Oh . . . about three month.' At this, Annie tsked and rolled her eyes. Three months was *ages*.

The gardener considered for a moment. 'Hold out your hands.' With his fork he turned over a patch of earth, then pulled up a somewhat tatty leek and dropped it in Annie's hands. 'Give your mam that,' he said. Annie was delighted to have been deputised, and this might have been what made her squeal, though it was hard to tell because Annie was forever squealing. In any case, she galloped off towards the Hall with the leek.

The gardener's name was Sam Hobbs. He was unworldly in all things except human nature, which was all that really counted, and in such matters he was wise. His experience, by the measure of a standard man, had been limited, but he had fully experienced every bit of it, which he reckoned made the odds even. He could boast no great depth of learning, but faced down life's trials as they presented themselves through graft, pluck, and a handful of judiciously composed habits. In a group of equals he was seldom the first or the last to speak. Given a list of jobs to do, he began with the least pleasant. He knew that getting something for nothing was, at some level, everybody's plan because, at some level, it was his plan too.

While Izzy mooched about at the edge of the vegetable patch, Hobbs ceased work and smoked a pipe. This is quickly said but it was not quickly accomplished. First, he removed the clay pipe from his breast pocket, and then he produced a thin-bladed penknife and used it to scrape out the ashes of his previous smoke, keeping the ashes cupped in one palm while gently tapping the pipe against his thigh to remove the last of the burned baccy or any other muck that had collected there. Next, he had to locate his baccy pouch. To his surprise, he felt Izzy's unblinking gaze making him uneasy, so he asked her her name, and having learned what it was, asked what she thought of Eshwood Hall. Izzy said that it was all right, she supposed. The pouch having been located, Hobbs cut a piece from the black plug of tobacco, refilled the bowl of his pipe and tamped it down. Then he placed the ashes on top of the fresh plug. He asked Izzy a few more questions, and so he learned that the Whippers had moved to Eshwood from Ubbansford, where her dad had worked down the pit at Butterlaw, which he'd hated, and before that they'd lived in Seven Springs, where her dad had worked as a stonemason's mate, putting up drystone walls mainly, which he'd loved but Mam had hated because there was no one to talk to, and before that they'd lived in Betlashield where her dad worked in a garage, fixing cars and things. Hobbs took in all this and more while finding his matches and finally getting his pipe lit to his satisfaction, and then he puffed away contentedly and waited for Izzy to get around to saying what she was thinking of saying.

'Do you believe in ghosts?'

'Believe . . .' repeated Hobbs, as though he had never heard the word before, and then, 'Well, I cannot say I do, and I cannot say I don't. You might say I've apprehended some things I cannot explain. I suppose anotherbody might be minded to call them ghosts.'

'Like what?'

'Oh, I've heard some things and seen some things . . .'

Izzy recognised that he was playing for time, but she was patient.

'Well, you'll have heard tell of the Grey Lady? I saw her one time.'

Izzy had not heard about the Grey Lady, but of course she wanted to, and said so. Hobbs was poking some more baccy into his pipe.

'It was back in twenty-six or twenty-seven, when Colonel Claiborne was lord of the manor, and I was just started here, as a stable lad. The job hardly paid nowt, but it came with a room, and that's what I needed most just then. Green as I was, I knewed something was up when I saw the room they'd given us: it was thrice as big as I'd any reason to expect, and – well, not *fancy* exactly, it was a bit too shabby for that, but it had *used* to've been fancy. There was a table, and an old press against one wall, but they were as nowt in such a big room, and in one corner there was this four-poster bed. I couldn't believe it: I'd never even seen a four-poster before, let alone slept in one. I even asked if they'd got the right room, but, "No, no, it's yours if you want it," they said. So I said I did and that was it and all about it.

'So I did my day's work, and the boss, Mr MacDevitt, he

34

was a devil of a gaffer – used to call us Blister because he said I turned up after the work was done – mind you, to be fair, once the war got started he wangled a way to get hisself signed up, though he needn't've, he was too old for the draft, and he ended up getting taken prisoner and put on the Burmese Railways . . . and anyways, I gets to bed so tired that when I blew the candle out I was asleep afore the room got dark.' His eyes twinkled and Izzy giggled. 'Anyways, I gets to sleep straight off, being so tired, but, wouldn't you know, I woke up in the wee hours, and I was completely unable to get back to sleep. The bed had grown a new set of lumps while I'd been kipping, and every other spring seemed to be poking and jabbing at us like MacDevitt's fat finger when he thought I wasn't working hard enough. On top of that, I was freezing cold: absolutely nithered! Well, I knew that I wouldn't be getting another wink o' sleep that night. And that's when I saw her.'

Here, Hobbs broke off to relight his pipe. Once this was done, and he had all but disappeared in pale blue smoke, he continued.

'I was lying there trying to find a comfortable patch on the mattress, and I hears this queer sound. At first, I thought it was mice in the rafters, and then I thought it was rats under the floorboards, but no: it was the doorknob turning and slipping back and turning again. By now I was wide awake, o' course. I don't know why I didn't call out, but I didn't, I kept my peace. Eventually, the knob got turned enough to catch, and the door opened a keek. Straight off, there was this queer green glow from t'other side of the door. I watched while the door slowly, slowly opened – and you might think it'd creak, but no, it swung silent – and there she was stood.'

'The Grey Lady!' gasped Izzy, but Hobbs didn't answer, he just briefly raised his eyebrows over his pipe, and then continued.

'She was all dressed in a grey cloak with a hood, and you couldn't see her face, 'cause the hood was pulled right over, and she had her head down. The green glow was coming from under the hood.' Izzy's eyes widened at this revelation. 'Ever so slowly she moved across the big room towards us. I remember I couldn't see her feet, 'cause the cloak was so long, and I couldn't see her hands, 'cause she had her arms folded, like. She slid over the floor like a chess piece over a board, but slowly. And then, without saying a word, she started tucking us in! First one side, then t'other, slow as you like, and I just lay there, it was like I couldn't move. And though she was just a little body, she was strong as a ox, and she tucked us in so tight I could hardly catch me breath. Both sides she did, and then the bottom, and all the while the blanket was tight on me chest like I don't know what. And when she was done, she stood at the foot o' the bed – arms folded, head down, with that green glow still coming out from under the hood – and she just stood there and waited. And I knew she was going to wait until I got away back to sleep. And do you know, I *did* feel sleepy again, and comfortable enough, apart from the tightness of the blankets on my chest. And I'd have thanked her, except I couldn't hardly catch me breath to speak, so I didn't. I just shut me eyes, and before I knew it, I was back to sleep again.'

Hobbs took another puff on his pipe.

'Well, I woke up next morning, still tucked in canny tight, mind, and went down for breakfast, and there's MacDevitt and Mrs MacDevitt, and little Jimmy Cowie and all, and they're all looking at us wide-eyed. They cry, "What was up wi' ye last night?" And "How's that?" says I, and they cry, "Well, ye made such a racket like ye were being mordered!" I says, "I never!" but I could see by MacDevitt's face that he wasn't funning, he was dead serious. And I never told them about the Grey Lady, 'cause they'd've thought I was soft, but I tell you, that was the last night I spent in that room, and the last night anybugger spent in it as far as I'm aware.'

Altogether, this was the most amazing thing Izzy had ever heard. She watched Hobbs relighting his pipe while she considered the facts. Eshwood Hall was haunted, that much was evident. She had half-suspected it would be. She would have to be prepared in case the Grey Lady came to tuck her in. Should she warn Annie about the Grey Lady? She wouldn't decide just yet.

'Did Mr MacDevitt know there was a Grey Lady when he gave you that room?' she asked.

Hobbs looked at Izzy and his eyebrows fell. 'I reckon he did. I reckon he'd heard tell of it, but didn't thoroughly believe it, so he sends me in to see if there was owt to it.'

Izzy expressed her view that Mr MacDevitt shouldn't have let him sleep in the room if he knew about the Grey Lady, and Hobbs observed that he'd never spent another night in the Hall since, explaining that he lived in one of the cottages across the way, preferring to keep himself to himself and leave things such as the Grey Lady to themselves and that was the way he saw it, anyway.

There was only one thing left to find out: which room had Hobbs seen the Grey Lady in? Izzy asked, but Hobbs just looked away and said he couldn't remember. Izzy looked at him – he scratched the back of his head – and she wondered.

3

In what was already understood to be her chair, Gerry was adrowse. The grandmother clock ticked solemnly but soothingly: *Now/then*, it said, *now/then, now/then* . . . The last cup of tea that Izzy had made for her stood cold on the coffee table nearby, and the Bairn slept on a blanket on the sofa, within reach, so close she could hear his soft breathing. Gerry valued her afternoon nap, the only five minutes she had to herself, and God knew she needed them. She watched the Bairn give a sigh and relax even further into his sleep, and she felt the tension releasing from her shoulders and her eyelids growing heavy . . .

Nothing Gerry had experienced raising Izzy and Annie had prepared her for little Raymond. He was, she knew it at first sight, the love of her life. Every mother had her favourites. Most fathers had a favourite as well, but all mothers did. Anyone who said otherwise was kidding somebody, probably themselves. She herself had been her parents' favourite. There hadn't been much of an attempt to hide the fact, either; with her the only girl after six boys, it was to be expected. People didn't make such a fuss about things back then, and you could almost say that it suited her brothers, as it ensured that they were all on an equal footing. With each other, that is. She had evened things out, as it were, and there was a sort of symmetry here, with little Raymond coming after the two girls, and long after she'd stopped thinking there would be another baby . . .

Why was having a boy so different? Gerry didn't know. It just seemed to change everything, and make her realise what she hadn't been feeling before. What she'd been putting up with, in a way. She was fascinated by this little man, whom she looked at so searchingly, learning his every expression, watching the silly doings of his fingers, burying her nose in his hair and sniffing the buttery smell of the crown of his head. There was a fire in her now. She finally understood what other mothers had been wittering on about. She was, she supposed, complete.

The sudden, insistent sound of a bell woke her with a start.

'Ray! Ray?' She looked confusedly around the room. The Bairn had awoken, and was regarding her with the expression of one sagely preoccupied. The bell was ringing again – a mocking sound it had – but she couldn't tell where the noise was coming from. From the window, she could hear Ray talking at Hobbs, though she couldn't see them. Neither of them seemed to have heard any bell. The place could be on fire for all she knew. It rang again, continuously. It seemed louder in the kitchen end of the parlour. She knelt down on the flags and leaned in closer to the range. The sound seemed to be coming from it, or from somewhere near it. She opened the nearby cupboards but found nothing; she even yanked open the bottom oven in the range. There was a board next to the range separating it from the nearest cupboard. She put her fingertips against it. The ringing sound came again, and she jumped, then pulled the board away from the wall. Behind it there was a small bell attached to a string that disappeared off between the floorboards.

'Christ in heaven!' Gerry grabbed the clapper between thumb and forefinger to silence the infernal thing.

It was at this moment that Ray appeared, and seeing his wife on the floor, of course he panicked, what with her having a weak heart and everything. 'Gerry, pet! What's the matter?'

Gerry budged over, revealing the hidden bell, which, released, commenced ringing again. '"It'll be peaceful," he says!'

Ray examined the bell. He looked impressed. 'Must be rigged all the way up to the old lady's room.'

'It's outrageous. This is our *private* space. I want it out, Ray!'

'The string must be run through a tube. I'll ask her not to ring it.'

'Oh, you'll *ask* her?'

'Now, pet, we've got to—'

Just at this moment, Hobbs repeated his trick of bringing peace to the Whippers by appearing unexpectedly in the doorway of their apartments.

'Isn't this a marvel!' said Ray from the floor, as though they were delighted to have discovered the bell. 'All the way from Miss Claiborne's room down to us here. Got to be four hundred yards.'

Hobbs observed that Miss Claiborne liked her bells and whistles. Although his line of work kept him at one remove from his employer, he nevertheless understood – and he now intuited that Ray did not understand – that to make a success of service requires equal parts sarcasm and reverence. It was already too late for Ray to learn this, supposing he were capable of learning, and so the Whippers' term at Eshwood Hall would not be a long one. So much he gathered in the time it took for Gerry to grunt at his little joke: his wiles were wasted, but not entirely thrown away, on Eshwood's three hundred acres.

Gerry couldn't get a good look at him as he was standing in the doorway blocking the light. 'Professor Peabrain showed you his inventions yet?' she said, by way of a hello.

Hobbs gave her a look that might have been one of appraisal. He certainly wasn't going to react to what she'd said otherwise. He found himself regarding her mouth – she had a way of sort of jutting her chin out when she spoke to you – and he wondered briefly what it would feel like to cradle her face and run your thumb over her soft cheek and the angle of her jawline. A moment later the bell rang again, and Ray said that that was him summoned, he supposed, and that he'd heard that a good servant came when he was needed, not when he was called for (which only confused matters since it didn't apply in this case) so he'd better get to work, and Gerry waved him away, so the two men left.

From the window Gerry watched Hobbs let himself out by the servants' entrance and make his way across the courtyard. The sun was blinding.

4

Miss Claiborne was sitting up in bed, arms by her side, palms pressed down firmly as though she feared a sudden gust of wind might whip the bedsheets up into the air. Did she ever sleep? She did not. She couldn't remember the last time she had truly enjoyed a night's sleep; and her dreams, as though they had given up on her ever sleeping again, now swam freely in and out of her waking memories. The bed she sat in, and the room, and indeed the entire Hall, were all inconveniently large for her needs. A mantlepiece like a cenotaph rose around a small fire that cracked and sputtered in the grate, too far away to warm Miss Claiborne, or anyone else.

Ray waited on the threshold, holding his hat, looking about at the vast room which was wainscoted with finely polished black oak and decked out with family portraits and dim mirrors, its curtains and upholstery pale green.

The family's living matriarch squinted at him from her bed. 'Whipper?'

'Yes . . . here, ma'am.'

'"Miss Claiborne" will do: I'm not her majesty the Queen!'

'Yes, Miss Claiborne.'

'I'm not blind either. I can see that you're there.'

'I'm reporting for duty, Miss Claiborne.'

'And I'm not a sergeant major. I take it you saw some action?' she asked as though the war had ended a week ago.

'Eighth King's Royal Irish Hussars,' Ray said promptly. He'd had a feeling that the war would come up.

'Ah! Most satisfactory. And I hope you gave the Boche a run for their money?'

'To tell you the truth, I spent most of the war repairing engines – in the jeeps and the tanks and what-have-you. After Sandhurst—'

It has to be admitted that at the mention of this place, this institution, Miss Claiborne failed to keep the incredulity quite out of her expression, and indeed quite out of her tone. 'You went to Sandhurst?'

'Yes, Miss Claiborne. Teaching the men how to drive, and that.'

'Oh, I see. You *worked* at Sandhurst.'

'Aye. Yes. Teaching the men how to drive. And I'll tell you one thing I noticed: it's twice as much bother to teach an educated man how to drive, because he'll want to know how it all works. He won't do a thing he's told until he knows what the engine's doing, and what's the difference between a stub axle and a steering swivel, and what-have-you. Whereas it's much easier to teach a man with no learning at all: he takes to it straight off. "Just press on this, and pull on that" – and he does as he's told, no questions, and before you know it, he can drive.'

'I see. Well, you will have no difficulty in looking after the motor should it play up. And you will be taking me to church twice a week, once I'm feeling better. Now, I understand you have a wife, Mr Whipper?'

'I certainly do: Gerry.'

'As in Geraldine?'

'Oh, she wouldn't thank you for calling her that, Miss Claiborne!'

Miss Claiborne managed to raise her eyebrows even higher at this. She'd been living in this phase of her life for decades. Although seldom seen by the people of Eshwood village, she was often thought of; but she was steadily losing ground to what she had come to represent. Each day she stepped deeper into the legend that would outlast her, one of absolute propriety and a haughty brand of *noblesse oblige*. She wasn't used to chatty men like Ray. She would think carefully before deigning to meet the other Whippers.

'She'll be "Mrs Whipper" to me, I can assure you. Though why anyone should be so unhappy with the name of Geraldine is rather mystifying. Is she . . . is she *young*?'

'She's two year older than me, Miss Claiborne, and always will be.' Miss Claiborne appeared to be scandalised, in a small way, to hear this, but Ray carried on unperturbed. 'And we have three young-ones: Izzy, she's the oldest, just turned thirteen, and Annie, she's eight, and there's the Bairn of course, little Raymond, he's just four months old.'

'Well, you're here now. I hope you're all settling in, as they say. Sheila should be able to tell you anything you need to know. Do remember to close and lock the outer door every night: that's one of your responsibilities. Now, I have a more immediate job for you, Whipper . . .'

Unable to stop himself, Ray stood to attention.

'I want you to see to the brace of woodcock that are hanging in the woodshed. Last of the season, so have a care with them! I want you to pluck them, and take them to Sheila: she'll take it from there . . .'

5

That evening Dad calls for Annie and Izzy and the way he does it makes Annie think she's going to get wrong but actually Dad just asks them if they fancy having a bit look round the Hall. Annie squeals and jumps up and down until Dad tells her howay and pack it in so she does. After that Annie and Izzy go with Dad to have a bit look around. It's excellent and there's a stable block which is excellent but they don't have any horses so the stable block's empty. The reason there aren't any horses is because they don't have a use for them Dad says. They might get horses in the future but Dad wouldn't get his hopes up. They have a look in the stable block anyway and Dad says they're allowed to play there if they want if they're good. Then they go back out and around and then they go in the front door to the Hall which is massive and the first thing they see is a ginormous staircase. Also there's an oval-shaped window in the roof right up a height. Annie's never seen a window in a roof before and can't see the point. You'd get a sore neck if you looked out of it for long. There's a room with loads of guns in it and Dad says he thinks he's seen a pheasant or two about the place so maybe Annie can earn a few bob when the season starts by being a beater though she'll have to learn to shut up for five minutes. Upstairs is loads of doors including the Big Door that connects this bit to their bit of the Hall. Annie and Izzy are allowed to look in the rooms as long as the doors are unlocked and they promise not to go spoaching so they promise. In one room there's a tiny piano called a clavichord.

It's called a clavichord but it's a tiny piano really. Some of the keys work and some of the keys don't work. It's like a grand piano except tiny. Annie can't play the piano and neither can Izzy but they both have a go and it makes a funny tinkly sound like it's far away or underwater or something. They take turns having a go. Dad says they can have a go as long as they behave though but. In one room there's these black satin screens with all these designs on them in gold thread. Dad says they're probably from India and Annie says where's India and he tells her. They're quite horrible actually because they're so threadbare and dusty. Annie asks what they're for and Dad says for hiding behind. In one room there's nothing but loads of old brown battered suitcases and Annie and Izzy have a look to see what's inside them and the suitcases are full of books and the books look as old and battered as the suitcases. Dad looks at the books and says Charles Dickens. Annie asks him why the books are in the suitcases and he says he hasn't a clue. Also in the room's a rocking horse except the paint's flaking off it and the mane is mostly baldy now and it's too scary. Annie says whose rocking horse is it and Dad says it must've belonged to the Claiborne bairns. Annie says where are they and Dad says they're dead. Annie reckons it'd be excellent to play games of hide-and-seek in the rooms but it'd be scary too if it was just her and Izzy because of the dead bairns and their rocking horse. They're probably allowed to play in the rooms though Dad hasn't totally said they can but he hasn't totally said they can't either. It's scary to think of someone jumping out from behind the dusty screens but it'd be excellent to jump out. There's other hiding places too like wardrobes and an ottoman which is like a wardrobe lying down. Then they see Sheila from the kitchen and she's going to the cellar for something and she says do yous want to see the cellar and Dad says aye why not if that's all right so they go to the cellar which is underground. The cellar has loads of old things in it like old furniture and old wooden frames and everything's cobwebby. Izzy and Annie have a good look around. The best thing in the cellar is a sundial that has precious jewels like rubies and sapphires and emeralds in it. There's a picture of the sun on it with loads of rays coming out and the rays are made of elephant tusks and all round the edges is funny squiggles and pictures like there's a picture of a crab and a picture of a scorpion and a picture of an ox and other pictures. Izzy runs her finger slowly over each of the pictures like she's drawing them and she has to draw them all. Sundials are meant for telling the time but they only work if they're outside and it isn't. It isn't outside because folk would thieve the precious jewels. Look Dad says you can see some of them's missing and there's scratches where a knife's been at them. Sheila says aye it was the soldiers when the Hall was used as a hospital during the last war like when the soldiers would say their prayers but one time a soldier said he was going to say his prayers but he sneaked away over to the sundial and pinched the diamonds out of it. Izzy stays looking at the sundial for ages but Sheila hangs about till she's finished and then Izzy has a bit more look around the cellar but it's boring apart from the sundial and Annie starts getting twisty and they all go back upstairs and they have a look at some of the downstairs rooms which Annie and Izzy and

Dad haven't had a look at yet. Sheila doesn't go with them though because Sheila has work to be getting on with. Sheila says one of the downstairs rooms is hers but she doesn't say which one. Annie asks which one but Sheila says mind your beeswax which means mind your business. In most of the downstairs rooms there's things under white sheets and it's spooky but when Annie and Izzy look under the sheets it's just old furniture. Sometimes there's other things as well as the furniture under the white sheets but sometimes there's just furniture under white sheets. If you were playing hide-and-seek you could hide under the sheets and all. Annie asks Dad if the furniture's antique and he says aye he supposes. Annie asks Dad if the furniture's precious and he says I doubt so. Then they go back through the Big Door and along the corridor to their rooms and Dad says he's going to put a bit music on but when he tries to put a bit music on he can't because the needle on the record player's broke. He's right mad because the needle's broke and he shouts at Annie and Izzy and wants to know who broke it but Annie and Izzy both say it wasn't them and swear and everything. Dad says he knows he didn't break it and he doesn't think it was the Bairn so that only leaves them. Then Annie says what about Mam. Jesus Christ says Dad. Mam starts laughing and Annie and Izzy try to join in laughing and all to try to make Dad see the funny side. Come on see the funny side says Mam. Look it's just a bloody needle Mam says it's not a bloody needle it's a bloody stylus Dad says.

3

The Chapel

Ray's capabilities as a chauffeur had not thus far been put to the test, but today might be the day: it was Good Friday, and Miss Claiborne was considering going to church. But really, did she feel up to it? She had yet to decide this. It was a fact that her sciatica had given her no rest since Palm Sunday. Indeed, she found that she could correlate many of her recent aches and ailments with events in the Christian calendar: she'd missed hanging the greens on account of pains in her chest; on Gaudete Sunday her earache returned with a vengeance; she'd had a bad cold for Christmas and on Epiphany an attack of vertigo; Ash Wednesday had brought a persistent headache. Just now she was eating the chuckie-egg that Sheila had brought her for breakfast. She'd see what she felt able to attempt after that.

Sheila was prattling about Mrs Whipper, and her evident lack of manners:

'She says to us, "When's the shop? Is there a weekly shop around here or what?" And I says, "How's that?" And she says, "Well, I want some bread." And I says, "I bake bread every Thursday! Every Thursday like clockwork! Just take a loaf up from the kitchen as and when!" And she says, "No," she says, "I mean proper sliced bread from the shop."'

While she spoke, Sheila was gesturing helpfully towards the bread on the side-plate; but Miss Claiborne's thoughts were elsewhere. Chuckie-egg always put her in mind of dear old Cook, whose name was Mrs Wardhaugh – though to the Claiborne children she had always been Cook or Cookie – and who had introduced them to the dish. But was it Francis or Cecil who liked it best? John liked kedgeree, of that she was certain. Sheila was gesturing again.

'Then she starts on about the butter. I says, "What's wrong with the butter? It's home-made!" And she looks at us and, "Aye," she says, "that's what's wrong with it: it's too farmyardy." I couldn't believe it, Miss Claiborne! I says, "Too farmyardy? That's not even a proper word!" Then she likened it to a cow-blake, only she didn't say "cow-blake". Honestly, to hear her on – she'd make a navvy blush, Miss Claiborne, she really would.'

Miss Claiborne watched Sheila throw a shovelful of coal on the fire, straighten with an expressive sigh, and wipe her hands on her apron. Sheila was stout, Miss Claiborne thought. A stout little loaf. The staff of life. She was staff. Cookie had been staff as well, of course, but had never felt like staff.

'She says, "I tell you another thing: I cannot abide this milk you've got here." I says, "Woman, it comes straight from the cow!" She says, "Aye, and that'd be bad enough in this day and age, but what makes it worse, you carry the stuff in old wine bottles!" I says, "Well, what's wrong with that?" And do you know what she said? She reckons it taints the milk.'

Miss Claiborne harrumphed at this, but it was an essentially rhythmic response that didn't necessarily indicate that its maker was listening.

'Well, to cut a long story short, in the end I refused. I just flat-out re*fused* to put bread on the list when there's plenty of it, and of a superior quality, available in the kitchen. If she wants a sliced loaf so badly she can go and buy it herself with her own money. What do you make of it? Have you ever heard the like?'

Miss Claiborne chewed meditatively on her last mouthful of bread. Real bread. The bread of the real, as she knew it. Replete, she surveyed the room and the situation objectively. 'I think,' she said, as though she had just made her mind up about something, though in fact she'd decided long before, 'I think that I shan't go to church today after all.'

2

Izzy was just dawdling along, savouring her freedom, following a rough sort of path that led into the woods. The

River Esh was somewhere near: the air was heady with the sparkle of running water. Maybe the path would lead to the river, or maybe it was a way through the woods, she didn't mind. Spring was finally getting started, and the alders were just coming into bud. Funny trees, alders: even in bud they looked half-dead, all scurfy and mossy. She had used to think (maybe she still thought) that alders were boys and birches were girls, but how did she know that? Had someone told her? She didn't remember. And of course, she knew trees weren't really boys and girls. When she was little she'd thought that all cats were girls and all dogs were boys, and had once argued the point forcefully with a boy at school called Melvin Fisher who was always picking on her. She hated Melvin Fisher, but when she'd asked Mam and Dad about it afterwards Dad had said Melvin was right, and Mam had called her soft, and said she didn't have the brains she was born with. Izzy hated Melvin Fisher even more after that. But that was ages ago when she still went to school. She missed going to school. It was queer, but she thought she even missed Melvin Fisher in a way.

The path she'd been following had led her deep into the woods and – Izzy's stomach gave a turn when she saw this – had now disappeared from under her. When she looked back the way she'd come, there was nothing like a path to be seen. How long had she been wandering among the trees? To be lost in the woods is to be lost in time, she thought, and wondered if she'd just thought it or if she'd heard it somewhere before. It was true anyway, because the time of trees was so much slower than the time of people; a moment in the real world might be a month in the forest. It was silent now as well, windless – and where had the sound of the river gone? She spun round looking for a landmark, and that's when she first saw it, a small building, half-hidden, but waiting to be found, waiting for her swimming gaze to settle on it.

As she drew closer Izzy could see it was a chapel of some kind, though evidently long since abandoned. The trees grew so close to its outer walls, their trunks rising up like pillars, that it looked, she thought, like a church inside a church. What would a body do in such a place, she wondered; whisper the prayer inside the prayer? Worship the god inside the god? She was standing before it now, and wanted very much to get inside, but soon found the front door wouldn't budge. Stepping back and craning her neck, she could see that the little bell-turret had three arched openings, and considered climbing up to see if she'd fit through ('If you can get your head and one arm through a gap, then you'll fit through it', Dad had told her once, and she'd stored the words away dutifully with other useful information), but then, at the back of the Chapel, she found another, smaller door, and it opened easily.

Inside, the floor was littered with leaves and pigeon droppings, and the air had been so long undisturbed that it seemed to have thickened and grown ponderous. There were seven rows of pews, a bone-dry font made of stone and yet apparently stained with rust, and, instead of a pulpit, a vast oak armchair carved with flowers and foliage. The roof was adorned with foliate heads – queer, ugly faces with branches sprouting from their mouths and noses, and sometimes from their ears and eyes as well – and also with carved angels holding shields. It looked to Izzy as though the angels and the foliate heads were ranged against one another like chess pieces. In the centre of the Chapel was a granite tomb – Izzy supposed it to be marble – inscribed with the name of Lord Somebody and a chain of Roman numerals. The sides of the tomb had canopied niches, in which stood the figures of young girls also holding shields, each dressed in kirtle, tunic and mantle. Between the stained-glass windows, a series of tombstones were let into the wall, and decorated with floral shields, swords, staffs and chalices. Above the door was an especially ornate foliate head with leafy branches coming from his mouth – oak leaves, Izzy saw, and among them acorns, though the cups were all empty – so that was the last thing you'd see as you left; and the first thing that you'd have seen when you entered that way was the crucifix on the opposite wall. Beneath the crucifix was carved the legend: *In your devotion you bring all that you came here to seek.* The crucifix and the huge foliate head seemed between them to generate a field of force; the air all but crackled.

Izzy knew what she was going to do. She was going to sit in the huge oak chair. Just for a moment. No one need know. Her footsteps crunched on the dry leaves and twigs as she crossed the floor. The Chapel was watching her, she could feel it. Izzy kept her eyes fixed on the chair – the throne – as though it were a living thing apt to take fright and gallop away before she reached it. Up close, it was if anything even more impressive, its elaborations soaked in the time and labour it must have taken to carve them, so that each detail seemed a power, a value demanding to be acknowledged. The whole thing had been polished, or waxed, and it had the dull shine of a rose hip. When she ran a finger along the throne's filigreed arm, she felt a thrill as though she'd touched a sleeping cat. There was something wrong here, but what was it? And suddenly – she almost laughed – she realised: it was such a little thing, but utterly mysterious: there wasn't a speck of dust on the throne, and yet everything else in the Chapel bore a layer of the stuff. Izzy bent closer. It was pristine, as though the workman had only just laid aside his chisel. Had someone been here, lately? It hardly seemed possible. It *wasn't* possible: they would have left a trail in the dust and debris on the floor. Izzy took a deep breath, turned, and sat down on the throne.

It was like putting on new knowledge. It was like a tree, struck by lightning, throwing off its bark. It was like in a dream when you realise you can fly, and so easily you can't believe you didn't have the knack before. It was like freedom from fear, absolute and terrible. It was like conveyance, like being portered through a strange landscape at incredible speed, being still and without agency or any especial feeling about the matter, but speeding along nonetheless, ever closer to the destination that awaited you. It was like looking through a powerful telescope and seeing a ship sink in the distant ocean, knowing there's nothing to be done about it. It was like being somehow simultaneously on the ship as well. It was like holding a lamp that held a genie, and also like being the genie inside; and it was like opening the lamp. And she could hear the distant applause of buds popping open on the branches of the beech trees in the wood. And she could hear the rent of the shell of a starling's egg as it hatched, and the first cry of the baby bird as it reared its blind, bristly head in a ragged nest built in the knothole of a pollard elm. And she could hear the gasp of the otter before it slipped beneath the surface of the trackless waters of the Esh. And she could smell on the west wind the last, half-smothered drift of woodsmoke from a charcoal-burner's grid-iron. And she could hear carried on the same breeze the whirr of the flywheel of the thresher in a barn. And she could smell the sweet, rotting marmalade odour of the beer-stained floor in the cellar of the Garland in Eshwood village. And she could taste the bitter succulence in the stems of the dandelions as they swayed in the sun. And now she was moving up and down and along her own veins with her own teeming blood.

She was lying on the floor with skinned knees. Had she thrown herself from the chair, or had it bucked and cast her off? Light-headed, she turned, half-crawling away to see if it had moved . . . No, there it was, where it had always been, all innocence, dumb as a water-butt. A chair. Izzy picked herself up and backed away. The light seemed different, as though she'd closed her eyes for a short nap and woken up in another part of the day altogether. She should be home already – there was washing to be done, that should be under way, and, she remembered, she didn't even know exactly where she was . . .

The everyday world was already bearing down on her, but she took a last look around the Chapel before she left. It was the best place she had ever been. Izzy knew then and there that she'd come back often and that she'd never tell anyone about it.

3

After all of her worry at getting lost in the woods, Izzy found her way back to the Hall quickly and easily – more quickly, in fact, than had seemed possible – and was home before the rest of the family had returned from church, so no one needed to know that she'd been out. She got straight on with a load of washing, lugging the laundry basket down the corridor to the poss tub the servants shared. Holding the dolly-stick with both hands, she pounded at the churning mass of long johns and nappies until an ache developed in her chest. It was nobody's fault, though. It was nothing – she'd just winded herself. But then she caught herself wondering: who *decided* if it was nothing? Was this what had happened to Mam? What if she'd got a pain in her chest after pounding clothes in a poss tub, and the doctor had seen her and said she had to take it easy for the rest of her life? What would happen if a doctor were to see Izzy? The questions kept churning. Izzy pounded at them.

Back in the parlour, Izzy shovelled some more coal onto the range, and heard the familiar sound of the Hawk rumbling up to the Hall, the crunch of gravel rhyming with the scoop in the coal. She set up the clothes horse and a couple of chairs before it, and had just started to hang out the laundry when the room became full of life once again: soon, Annie was seated at the table swinging her feet and drawing a picture of a horse jumping over a church, and Gerry was in her chair nursing the Bairn and flipping through an old copy of *Good Housekeeping*.

Izzy couldn't tell what sort of mood Mam was in. Annie was behaving herself, but that could mean that Mam had shouted at her earlier – or Annie could have been behaving herself all morning, and therefore Mam might be in a good mood . . . Izzy found that she was standing on her tiptoes. She peeked over Mam's shoulder at the title of the article, and read: 'What Women Should Know About Hormones'. She decided to ask a question.

'Mam, what's hormones?'

'According to this article I'm trying to read, you'll find out soon enough.'

This didn't help, as Izzy couldn't tell if Gerry was joking, or what was funny about it, so she tried again: 'Mam, can I ask you something?'

Gerry grunted a reply that didn't seem to indicate either yes or no. The Bairn was proving to be twisty – she'd given up on nursing him and was buttoning her blouse.

'I wanted to ask you – you never talk much about when you were younger, or when you were little, or before you had me – Dad talks about it, sometimes, but you don't, or at least not so much . . . and I wonder what things were like, and – well, I wanted to ask you something about your heart—'

'Why are you only just hanging them out?' Gerry asked suddenly. 'They should be dry by now. What have you been doing all this time?'

Izzy said that Wilkes had been using the poss tub, so she'd had to wait for him to finish. This wasn't true, but Izzy found that it came easily to the tongue and sounded as true as anything else she could have said. Then she worried that maybe Wilkes had been in church and that Mam had seen him, in which case she'd know that Izzy had lied, so she changed the subject by asking where Dad was.

'Where do you think? Straight back in his shed. Rat up a drainpipe.'

Some time passed in silence. When Izzy had finished hanging out the clothes, she found herself mooching around listlessly. Now she was attracting Mam's attention by just standing there and not saying anything. It was obvious that this would soon irritate Mam enough for her to say something about it, and if that happened, there would be even less chance of learning anything . . .

Gerry had stopped reading and was looking directly at Izzy, who blurted out, 'When did you first know that there was something wrong with you?'

'What a barrage of questions! Are you taking the census?'

'No, it's just I got a pain in my chest when I was washing the clothes—'

'That's just a pulled muscle. It doesn't mean anything.' Gerry turned back to her magazine.

'I know, but it made me think—'

'You hear that, Annie? Your sister's a thinker. A philosopher. Do you know what a philosopher is? Ask Izzy. She just pulled a muscle by thinking.'

'I know, but—'

'But nowt! Look: I have a heart condition, so you want one, too. I see how that works. Pain in your chest! Give me strength. It would be awful if I got to read this magazine in peace for five minutes, wouldn't it? It would be the end of the bloody world if I was allowed to read a magazine. Jesus Christ. Girl does some washing and next thing her heart's going to explode in her chest.'

'I was just wondering when you first knew—'

'It's probably just your boobs getting started. They'll be sore, all right, don't you worry. Wait till they're grown and you've got a bairn chewing on them, then you'll have a reason to feel sorry for yourself. Stop sniggering, Annie, or you'll get a clip.'

Izzy could feel herself blushing and turned away so Mam wouldn't see. She didn't say anything.

'Here, make yourself useful and feed him, would you.' Gerry threw down her copy of *Good Housekeeping*, handed over the Bairn, and left the room. The cover showed a picture of a young girl blowing soap bubbles.

Feeding the Bairn was one of the tasks that Izzy dreaded. She put him down for a moment, while she measured out the water, poured the tin of evaporated milk into it, and then mixed in a few tablespoons of sugar and gave it a good stir. Already she could feel her stomach squeezing, her throat beginning to close. She poured the slop into his bottle and found a teat. That was the easy part done. Getting it into the Bairn, and getting it to stay there, were the difficult bits.

For the next ten minutes Izzy was a mechanic tinkering with a hiccupping engine that spat and coughed its fuel back up and out; after that, there was a twenty-minute stretch in which the Bairn cried, screamed and shook his head as though he were being attacked. Izzy soldiered on, feeding him as best she could around his tantrum, trying to catch him inhaling, along with various other strategies to outwit him and force the bottle back into his mouth. It seemed as though everything he swallowed got sicked back up until it was impossible for Izzy to keep her hands from being coated in the viscous pablum. If Izzy claimed the final victory it was by attrition: the Bairn was, quite suddenly, asleep. She laid him, very gently, in his cot, and took herself to the bathroom to get cleaned up.

While Izzy was washing her hands, a funny thing happened: she found herself with an image in her mind of herself, years older, with a thickened, heavy body and breasts that were continuously oozing evaporated milk, and then everything went quiet, and she felt like she was looking through the wrong end of a telescope. She didn't know that she was going to be sick until the last second, and made it to the toilet bowl just in time.

4

Izzy had been lying in bed watching the full moon inch through the branches of the oak for what seemed like hours. Although she could not now recall with any preciseness the way to or from the Chapel, she didn't fret about struggling to find it again in the future: it seemed to her that it had all but led her into the woods, that it had wanted her to find it, and, she reasoned, it wasn't about to let her forget where it was. Sleep felt far away from her. Perhaps this was because the bedroom window looked out onto the forest, where so many creatures would be waking up for the night. Izzy was starting to feel that in some ways she, too, woke up after dark. She was fast becoming an expert on the night's progress – the varieties of night-time smells for instance: at twilight, there was the delicate smell of lady's bedstraw like new honey; at midnight, the musk-mallow held sway; at dewfall, the long-withheld perfume of the lime blossom breathed over Eshwood Hall. Or maybe it was there all the time, she just didn't notice it during the day?

Izzy reached for her book. The moon was full, more than bright enough to read by. She twitched open the curtains and lay with her back to the window, so that the moonlight shone over her shoulder on to the pages, and resumed reading *The Enchanted Wood* by Enid Blyton. She had read it before, of course; she'd read all of her books many times. Dad still hadn't taken her to the library in Eshwood Hall or asked if she was even allowed in. It was a babyish book really, and if you'd asked her in the daytime she wouldn't have admitted that she still enjoyed it. It was a plain green hardback edition, so at least it didn't *look* babyish: if anyone had seen her reading it, they wouldn't have known.

She started at the start, with the family moving to the country because the dad had got a new job, just like her family. And there were two girls – Bessie and Fanny – and a boy called Jo, and none of them were silly like Annie, and they were friends and they had adventures, and as soon as they saw the wood, they knew it was enchanted, because the rustling of the trees sounded like they were talking to one another, and saying 'Wisha-wisha-wisha!' and whispering secrets and things.

Izzy listened to the wind in the trees outside, and tried to hear the sound as *Wisha-wisha-wisha*, but it sounded more like *Whisht*. Later in *The Enchanted Wood* there would be Moon-face, and Silky the Pixie, and the Land of Take-What-You-Want, and the Country of Loneliness, and Dame Slap's School . . . But a feeling of dissatisfaction and embarrassment at all of that was settling on Izzy. After seeing the Chapel with its decorated roof and its wooden throne, the world of *The Enchanted Wood* seemed like a depleted, exhausted thing. The more she tried to force herself to read it, the more unreal she felt.

Just then, into this unhappy moment, the scratching noise insinuated itself, very quietly at first. Izzy looked up from her book. She had forgotten about the noises, but she wouldn't, she suddenly realised, forget about them again: she'd listen for them every night, her ears tuned to their frequency. Subtle as they were, they would pull her from her dreams. Everything was in order in the room: Annie slept on, the door remained sensibly shut, the boxes that hadn't yet been unpacked waited in a stack next to the chair. Had the noise come from her parents' room? It had stopped now, and her vigil wasn't accomplishing anything, so she turned back to her book. Again, she read for a few moments before hearing the sound again: it spun and spiralled, popped and cracked, fluttered and wowed . . .

She decided to try to ignore it, but she could feel her body bracing itself for an eruption of distorted music. She kept reading with all her might. There was silence again for a few moments, and then it returned: more of a long-drawn sound this time, like a groove being shaved into a length of wood. It was in the room with her now, surely. And it was as though the shaving of the wood released whispers, because she could hear those, too, a sort of cloud of whispers indecipherably intermeddled. But what were they saying, and who were they talking to, and how did they get inside the wood in the first place? There was something melancholy about them. It was sad to think of whispers imprisoned with no one to hear them.

Silence now, but she listened as hard as she could. This, surely, was the very room in which Hobbs had long ago seen the Grey Lady. It was a grim realisation, and one that Izzy would remember the next day. There was a long pause and then the sound came again. This time the whispers seemed even closer on their release, as if they were in the room with her: *I-ss-s-ss-isz-ss-sz-i-p-eh-ll-ahh-ah-h* . . . Her eyes widened. They were saying 'Isabella'. They were calling her name.

4

The May Queen

All the housewives of Eshwood had scoured their doorsteps the night before, and today each step shone as bright as the red and yellow flags of Northalbion that hung from their windows. The only public house in the village, the Garland, was enjoying its busiest day of the year. It was said that the Mayor of Meldon, Mr Graham, would visit Eshwood later that afternoon, and a chair had been reserved for him at the judges' table, so that he could bestow the winners' rosettes during the agricultural show. Collars were starched, shoes comprehensively polished, hats debuted. This, according to the old calendar that Eshwood still used, was May Day.

Outside the Garland, although he never took a drink himself, Reverend Marshall was holding court.

'Now, the good book says to love thy neighbour, and that sounds simple enough, all right; but what if your neighbour is a real swine? What if, for example, he borrows money and doesn't pay it back? What if he bears false witness against you? The best Christian service you can perform is to apprise him of the fact, and of the fact that, as is invariably the case, word has got round and nobody likes him. For honesty is a Christian virtue as well, let's not forget. And the surest and fastest way to persuade such a one of his unlikeable habits may be, and in some circumstances *must* be, to raise your hand to him, and bust his nose. I say this as a servant of the Church. For in doing so you'll be giving him the chance to see the error of his ways, you see, or at least turn the other cheek and learn some humility. "Love thy neighbour" doesn't mean you have to put up with any old nonsense he throws at you, certainly. To let him carry on as such would be to do the Devil's work for him.'

Reverend Marshall had realised early in life that he'd a rare gift for extemporising sermons: ideas came to him all the time, too many to write down, and no need to write them either, because he could stand before his flock at a moment's notice and give forth the Lord's word – straight, filtered, or fancied up, as the occasion required.

It was at around this time that the Whipper family arrived, having walked the two miles from Eshwood Hall. They joined the crowd of spectators that were gathering around the green, feeling pleasantly anonymous despite being newcomers to the village, as everyone's attention seemed occupied elsewhere. In fact, Reverend Marshall had already glimpsed them and recognised them as the new faces at his Good Friday sermon; he was now making his way over to introduce himself properly, and find out what he could about these new members of his flock.

The Whippers had settled in to their new lives in Eshwood Hall, to the extent that this day out would feel like a day properly away from 'home', and they would be glad to get back there again when it was over. Had she been asked, Izzy would have said that she didn't mind living at the Hall. She had no say in the matter anyway, so there was no point in deciding she didn't like it there; and in truth she loved living so close to trees again. It had been ages since they had lived somewhere near a wood, and this one had the hidden Chapel, of course, which she had been to a number of times in recent weeks, always keeping her visits secret, her absence excused by a story of some sort. Every time she went there, she sat in the throne; but frustratingly, it had never had the same effect as it did that first time, when she'd felt so transported and had such mysterious thoughts and sensations. On every subsequent visit, it had always just been a big wooden chair. But it was curious that she had still not been able to pin down the Chapel's exact location: instead, the mood would take her, and she would slip out unobserved to go for a walk in the woods, and before she knew it, she had stumbled upon the place again and was letting herself in the back door.

Now, in the centre of the green, twenty or so boys and girls were dancing around a Maypole: each child held a coloured ribbon, and as they wove in and out between each other the colours braided together and crept in a forming mesh down the pole. The children clearly took their work seriously – their expressions were surprisingly solemn – but they danced so nimbly in between each other that the structure seemed to pulse like riverbed fronds and weeds in a current. The pattern the implicated ribbons made on the pole formed multicoloured diamonds, and when the top half was covered, as at a signal (though Ray had heard no signal) all of the boys stopped moving and held their ribbons still. Ray could see how it worked now: boys alternated with girls, so all they had to do was move in and around each other in the right order, and the overall pattern would take care of itself. Now that the boys were standing still, the girls began a more complicated dance around them, doubling back around each boy, so that the ribbons above them began to form a webby tent. The pole itself, Ray noted, was shoogly, and had to be held steady by two older boys, who crouched at its base and braced it with their shoulders. Just at the point when the children were about to be engulfed by the descending tent of ribbons, all of the girls stopped moving as well. Ray marvelled at how they seemed to do this all at once, by instinct. The dance must have been rehearsed many times, because the next movement seemed especially complex: all of the children resumed dancing, but this time they retraced their steps so that the web of ribbons opened out and unwound, revealing, at the end of the dance, which received a round of applause, two figures who had not been standing by the Maypole before: a man who looked to be in his sixties, and a girl of about Izzy's age, or younger, for Izzy was so small. The child dancers bowed and curtseyed and, for the first time, some giggled with what seemed relief that their part in the celebrations was over. But Ray was fascinated, because he couldn't for the life of him work out how these two new figures had been smuggled into the ring in the midst of such a busy dance. The old man was stripped to the waist, and his body and face had been painted all over green. He wore a wreath on his head, and a sort of waistcoat made of leaves or perhaps it was green paper – Ray wasn't close enough to be sure which – and he had more leaves and twigs sticking out of his beard. The girl wore a white dress that might have been silk (Ray was uncomfortable to see how sheer it turned in the sunlight, but nobody else seemed to notice), and a tall crown made of carefully inwrought flowers and blossoms. They certainly made a queer couple, Ray thought, and this was accentuated by the way the old man was grinning rather inanely while the girl looked entirely serious.

The old man took a step forward and raised his hand as the last of the applause died away. Beaming, he declared in a tenor:

> *Married in May and kirked in green,*
> *Bride and groom won't lang be seen!*

This received another round of applause. Seeing Ray's bewilderment, Reverend Marshall, who had been standing next to him all this time, introduced himself, and explained that the Maypole dance had revealed this year's Jack in the Green and May Queen. Reverend Marshall also explained that Eshwood village was the exact geographic centre of Britain, and that the Maypole was the centre of the village: the coordinates were there, on a sign above the door to his

Methodist church. By the emphasis that Reverend Marshall gave the denomination, Ray intuited a history of rivalry between him and whoever was the priest at St Jude and All Souls – Father Lawrence, wasn't it? Still, this business with the coordinates was just the sort of information Ray liked to know, and he would enjoy passing it on to Gerry as soon as he could.

Unseen by her father and unregarded by anyone else, Izzy had been watching the Maypole dance closely from another part of the crowd. The May Queen fascinated her. She was the most beautiful girl she had ever seen. Her hair was, Izzy thought, like spun gold; her skin pure as cream. Izzy really had nothing to liken her to but damsels from fairy tales. Her heart gave a squeeze, and she felt a moment's terrible yearning to be the May Queen's friend – her best friend, her only confidante – and to brush her golden hair. A series of tableaux flickered across her mind's eye, plucked from silly stories and sillier songs, and it was all over as soon as it had begun and she'd tell no one.

Jack in the Green took the May Queen by the hand and now they stepped forward from the Maypole. A pony trap had been brought along: it was entirely festooned with flowers, and instead of a pony there were four boys in white silk costumes to pull it along. The couple slowly approached their chariot, and climbed inside. Jack was a gentleman, of course, and allowed the lady to enter first, holding her hand daintily, grinning at the crowd. And then, after Jack had waved a whip of sweet peas wound along a string, the team of boys set off at a trot, taking the couple on a circuit of the village green.

Once the circle was completed, the trap headed off towards the Garland, and the crowd broke up as families drifted towards the market stalls. The Whippers made their way over towards the hog roast. They were queuing for so long that Annie was twisty by the finish, but at last they were served and Ray and Gerry got a hog roast stotty and Gerry gave some to Annie so she piped down. After that Izzy and Annie went off exploring. The first thing they saw was a man hacking a large log into the shape of a squirrel, using only his axe. He accomplished this astonishingly quickly, for he was well practised, having done it every May Day for nigh-on forty years. The second thing they saw was a group of women dancing in wooden shoes, which Annie thought was funny but Izzy said it wasn't meant to be. The third thing was a boxer limbering up: he was shirtless so you could see how barrel-chested he was, and he had a flat nose and a waxed moustache. He stood next to a sign that read 'All Comers: 1/6 per round', but as there were no takers he was lighting a cigarette. Families were picnicking on the outskirts of the green, and people were browsing the stalls of vegetables and cheeses and jams. At each one, the farmer had his most impressive specimen of vegetable set apart, not for sale but for the prize-giving later.

Izzy found herself looking for something to buy for Mam. She didn't have any money, so she wouldn't be able to actually get anything; if anyone had asked her, she'd have said that she was window-shopping, and been glad of the chance to use the phrase, for she felt that it held an attractive air of mystery. Mam was difficult to buy for in any case: for her last birthday, she'd received from Izzy a set of six small glasses, hardly bigger than a thimble, each one a different colour. Izzy had loved looking at them, so bonny in a row, catching the light. Her favourite was the purple one – such a rich, royal colour, so plum full of itself, so plush! Izzy had been saving her pennies for the best part of a year to get Mam a birthday present. She'd received three shilling for her birthday from Nana Whipper; she'd been given a half-crown by Pat next door for doing various odd jobs; and, incredibly, she'd once found a ten-shilling note just lying in the road. Her secret savings had accumulated, and as soon as she saw the glasses, she knew she had to get them. The woman in the shop had wrapped them in tissue paper and everything. But as Mam was unwrapping them later that evening, Izzy began to see that she'd made a mistake somewhere; maybe it was the way Mam didn't take her time with the paper, didn't seem to notice how pretty it was in its own right. Gerry had looked at the shot glasses with an expression that a grown-up might have described as embarrassed but which looked to Izzy like annoyance. And where had Izzy found the money to pay for them? Izzy told her. *How* much had they cost? Izzy told her.

Gerry regarded the shot glasses again in the light of this information. 'They must have seen you coming,' she had said.

*

Back on the village green, Ray slowly swayed the Bairn in his arms, as though they were dancing. Raymond Junior bobbed up and down, watching the crowd of people with an expression as grave and serious as that of the child dancers earlier. Gerry heard herself say, 'He doesn't . . .' but couldn't remember how she was going to complete the sentence, so let it trail off. The sun was really getting out now. She fixed her expression and surveyed the locals in much the same way Mayor Graham would shortly inspect the competition marrows. Where had Ray landed them this time? Centre of Britain? Dead centre of nowhere more like. Not that it seemed to bother Ray – he looked happy as a clam! She considered her husband as he grinned encouragingly at their son. They had been married twelve years, though they never celebrated their anniversary, and always added two years to the tally if anyone asked. The fact was (it was a lifetime ago and Gerry never thought of it) she'd been married before, to a rat called Henry Fowler. It was clear to her now that she'd been little more than a child then – a spoiled child at that, some might say, with all those older brothers to fuss her . . . She grew up trusting the world to look after her and provide the comfort to which she'd grown accustomed. Comfort, that is, not in terms of money or nice things – her family were poor as church mice, she freely acknowledged it; it would never be money that she was looking for, exactly – but in terms of being made to feel special and loved. In other words she was green when she came of age, and had said yes to the first man who'd had the gumption to ask. With her deep red hair that she kept long – all men liked that, she now knew, just as they all thought that they'd be the first to compare her to Rita Hayworth – she was a beauty; so much so in fact that she must have scared a lot of men off, but she hadn't appreciated this at the time, in her poor little half-hour of girlhood, and, not realising what a prize she was, she'd squandered herself on – it turned out – a rotten bastard who drank, and beat her. And for nearly three years it had seemed that was that: she'd be walled in alive with the mess she'd made of her first real decision.

But Ray had got her out. It was all secret, of course – Ray was meant to be courting somebody else as well – all furtive meetings and passionate agreements and thrilling doubts. The only time in her life that she'd a reason to be subtle. And then with Izzy on the way, she knew she'd have to choose and this time it really would be once and for all. Listening to Ray, anything seemed possible. They'd run off together and she'd get divorced and they'd get married and move north and that would be that. And that *is* what had happened, only it had all taken longer than either of them could have anticipated, and it was a bit of a scandal so they'd left Sheffield and kept moving until Ray picked up some work in a garage. They wouldn't let her marry in white again, the sods, so she'd worn a yellow dress. To hell with them. Gerry had referred to her ex-husband on precisely two occasions since the divorce, and both times had called him by his surname, which she was *delighted* to be free of. Her children did not know that she had been married before; she couldn't see how it was any of their business. Ray was nothing like Fowler. Ray was taller and better-looking for a start. And he liked dancing! The price to be paid was him shifting jobs every year, and them barely having a pot to piss in. It would have driven another woman mad, Gerry supposed, but whatever romance security and money might have held for her had been scrubbed off by the memory of Fowler's entitled drunken rages, of how quickly she'd learned to gauge his mood by the sound of a slammed door . . . Now here she was, wherever the hell this was, and there wasn't even anywhere to sit down.

'Isn't there anywhere to sit down?'

'I think you're meant to just sit on the green, pet.'

'In this frock! I don't think I'll be doing that. Can't we sit outside that pub?' Gerry nodded towards the Garland. It had benches outside, though all were currently occupied.

Ray hesitated for a second.

'Don't be a prude, for heaven's sake. I only mean outside. It's a *country pub*. I won't go in the taproom. I won't talk to anyone, don't worry!'

'Shandy, is it?'

'A glass of sherry. Grant's Regency Cream. If they've got it.' Gerry took the Bairn up in her arms and waited for Ray to set off towards the pub. But he just stood there like a pudding so she turned and stomped off herself. Ray hurried after her.

Gerry held the Bairn and waited outside the door marked 'Bar & Taproom – Men Only', and Ray disappeared inside. She was standing fairly close to one of the occupied benches. An animated man, talking, stepped backwards and bumped into her, and, catching her frosty stare, begged her pardon. When Gerry said it was quite all right the man said, 'I'm sure it is,' and his friends laughed dutifully. It would have made anybody cross, so Gerry asked pointedly whether they always made women stand while the men sat down, or if it was part of the May Day shenanigans.

'Do you want to sit down? Jimmy, shove over, let this bonny lass sit down.'

Jimmy shuffled closer to the man beside him, who looked disgusted and stood up. Gerry sat down and pulled the Bairn into her lap, who gazed at all the new faces wonderingly. Gerry looked uncomfortable but triumphant.

'Thank you.'

'My pleasure. And who's the little charva?'

'This is Raymond,' Gerry answered stiffly.

'Is he yours, is he?' the man asked amiably; to which Gerry asked why wouldn't he be hers, and the man, not liking to spell out the compliment, squirmed a little. 'You don't look like a lassie what's had kids.'

'I've had three, God help me!'

'Aye? You'd never know . . .'

This was all getting too familiar for Gerry's liking – not that she objected to friendliness, and of course, she was used to the effect she had on men, and yes, she was happy to gather their smiles and compliments and what-have-yous – but still she thought it only right to steer the conversation back to safer waters, and asked the gentleman, more pointedly than was perhaps necessary, how many children *he* had.

'Four. At the last count. Another one on the way.'

'Four that he knows of!' offered Jimmy.

'And where's your wife?'

At this, the man's expression finally soured. He nodded towards the green, and observed that his wife was sitting there, with the other hinnies.

'Hinnies! I'll never get tired of that one. Hinnies – like donkeys. Ray!'

Ray appeared holding a pint, and a half for Gerry. 'All right, fellas? Where do you want this, Gerry, pet? They didn't have any of that sherry so I got you a shandy after all . . .'

Gerry took her drink and tried to introduce the men, then realised that she only really knew Jimmy's name and nobody seemed to talk to him anyway. The man who had given her his seat turned out to be called Stephen, and he and Ray shook hands warily; and then Ray shook hands with Jimmy too, and then, since he'd done both of them, he shook hands with the other men in the group as well. Gerry sipped her shandy and the Bairn gurgled on her lap, while the men stood around uncomfortably, gradually turning their gazes back towards the green, where a troupe of Morris dancers was walking out and beginning to set up.

*

Annie was right glad to be at the May Day fair because there was loads of people there and loads going on and some people let you try a bit jam for free but she was also fed up because nobody was selling horses. They were selling sheep mainly and cows as well and pigs but not many pigs. If they'd been selling horses and all it would have been excellent and that's what she'd been expecting but no. Horses were Annie's favourite animal and she wanted a cob. She wanted a go on a Shire horse because they were the biggest but she wanted a cob. She'd only seen one horse at the whole fair all day and she'd thought it was a Shire horse but Izzy'd said it was just a draught horse. It was right good to see the horse even though it wasn't doing anything. Annie'd wanted to go over and pet the horse and maybe give it a carrot or something or see if she could have a sit on it but Izzy wouldn't go over because there was loads of men near the horse and she was chicken. If Annie could get a cob and it was black she'd call it Beauty and if it was brown she'd call it Bramble. She didn't know if she'd be able to get one though because they were a waste of money. After Izzy said she wouldn't take her over to pet the horse and that it got really boring so Izzy suggested Annie go back and find Mam and Dad and see what they were doing so she did.

*

Left to herself, Izzy moved carefully through the crowd, content to feel invisible; to hear scraps of jokes and talk, and smile as if she had been included; to imitate the faces of the buyers and sellers. If anyone wondered who this skinny little girl they had never seen before belonged to, they kept their concerns to themselves. She continued to circulate unregarded until she found herself joining the small crowd at the falconry exhibition.

There were three birds of prey standing on perches, and,

according to the falconer, they were a kestrel, a buzzard and a merlin. When Izzy looked more closely, she saw that they weren't just standing there, they were tied to the perches by a leather strap around their feet. The falconer was an unimposing man who wore a tweed suit and thick, black-rimmed spectacles. The most interesting thing about him was that he had a small, shaped beard and moustache, which made him look a bit like a magician, Izzy thought. She watched as he untied the leather strap around the merlin's feet, and let it fly off – it started heading in the direction of the Hall, but then started to climb and quite soon it had gone so far up that it disappeared from sight, and Izzy wondered how the man would ever be able to bring it back – and then he produced a lure from his pocket, and spun it in a circle a few times like a sideways lasso. Suddenly, the merlin swooped in from nowhere and caught it, bringing it down about ten feet away. All this time the falconer was telling everyone about how in olden times merlins and hobbies were the birds that ladies used for hunting, and how during the war they were used to keep gulls off RAF airfields. Izzy enjoyed watching the falconer retrieve the lure by giving the bird a piece of raw meat that he'd been carrying in a satchel. The merlin didn't want to give up the lure at first, and for a moment it looked as though it was going to attack the falconer. It didn't; but Izzy would remember the momentary thrill of the wild.

She became aware that she was being watched by the expressionless gaze of a boy. He was somewhat taller than her, with a pink face and broad shoulders and an unusually erect posture.

When he saw that she had noticed him, he wandered over towards her and announced, 'I'm Nodge.' Now, ordinarily, the boy would not have done this, and he had rather surprised himself by doing it, but this was May Day, and the air felt charged with licence that needed to be used up somehow, so why not talk to a girl? Izzy, who was so very unused to being in a crowd of folk, and so very used to being ignored, now felt even more at swim in this odd day. She had never heard of anyone called Nodge before, but didn't want to seem rude, so she told the boy her name was Izzy.

'It's *John* backwards,' Nodge explained, and then, 'I'm thirteen. How old are you?'

'Thirteen and all.'

Nodge regarded her. 'You don't look thirteen, like. You don't look eleven, hardly.'

Izzy assured him that she really was thirteen, and Nodge asked why in that case had he never seen her at school.

'I don't have to go to school. Mam has a weak heart and needs us to look after her.'

Nodge considered this. 'Next year's my last year anyway. After that I'll be helping Dad. He says there's no point in us spending all that time learning how to write italic when I could be making myself useful round the farm.'

Izzy enquired as to whether Nodge would prefer to stay on longer at school, and he shrugged. He said he had just had a go at hoy-the-welly and was now on his way to the village hall, where there would be dancing later. They'd be spreading the dance floor with salt about now, he said, and they always let the children in early to slide around on the salt and work it in for the dancers. Izzy couldn't follow the logic in this, but apparently you could slide around as much as you wanted, and see how far you could go, and it was muckle good fun in Nodge's opinion. It sounded good to Izzy so she decided to tag along with him.

On the way, she learned that Nodge's dad farmed a plot called Red Shield Farm for the Claibornes. Izzy asked why the Claibornes didn't farm it themselves and Nodge said his dad said it was because the Claibornes thought they were something they were not. They owned several neighbouring farms, which were all called Shields and given a colour: Blue Shield and White Shield and so forth. Izzy had an image of knights in armour fighting dragons, but Nodge said that 'Shield' came from 'shieling', which was a place where shepherds went to have a rest. Nodge was only allowed a bit of time off today and the rest of the time he'd be helping his dad with the beasts, so they hurried along to the village hall while Izzy heard again how much fun it was going to be to slide on the salt.

*

Back in the Garland, Ray and Gerry were getting to know the locals, or at least, some of the locals were getting to know them: Ray was doing his usual bit, talking nineteen to the dozen, while Gerry, notwithstanding her promise not to talk to anyone, had accepted an indeterminate number of shandies and was started to see the funny side of things.

At some point or other (it must have been when he was at the bar) she'd let slip that Ray was only getting paid £7 a week, and that Lady Muck was taking the cost of installing electricity in their quarters out of his wages, as he hadn't been able to do it himself. No doubt she shouldn't have said that, she reasoned, glancing defiantly around the room. They had watched the Morris dancers, or whatever they were – there were bells and tassels and drums and masks involved, and a sort of ridiculous dance, though the force with which the men whacked their clubs together seemed a bit overdone – and now Ray was telling the story about the woodcock, just as Gerry had known he would.

'So she says to us, "Whipper, fetch us thon brace o' woodcock," so I runs to fetch them where she says they're hung, and I can't find them, can I? And it's only then that I think on, and I say, "Wait a minute, woodcock's not in season the now, is it?" and I take myself off to find the cook—'

'*Chief* Cook,' interrupted Gerry, sniggering. 'Christ, *every*body's Chief Something-or-other up there . . . they all reckon they're something special . . .'

'Aye, the Chief Cook, that's right, I go and see her, and I tell her how I'm supposed to plote an invisible and out-of-season woodcock—'

'There's Big Chief Littlebum . . .'

'And the Chief Cook says, "Oh," she says, "pay her no mind, she doesn't know what month she's in!" she says —'

'And Little Chief Bigbum!' Gerry snorted.

'She says, "I'll make her some cheese on toast!"'

Truth be told, Ray had hoped for more of a reaction to

his story: it hadn't gotten much of a laugh. Gerry didn't help matters, eyes on anyone but him, engulfed by the attention of men whose names she barely knew, tapping her glass with her red fingernails every time it got empty. Or maybe he'd overstepped the mark by seeming to laugh at Miss Claiborne, him being so new to the area and all. It was so easy to make the wrong impression! So, by way of a hasty addendum, he made clear that he had nothing against Miss Claiborne or anyone: Miss Claiborne could eat as many imaginary woodcock as she liked. It had just struck him as funny, that was all.

And now at last Mayor Graham's black Morris Minor was pulling up to the village hall steps. The day was proceeding towards matters of business: claims had been staked by sellers, animals had been inspected by buyers, deals had been struck. The judges of the agricultural show – Mr Werge the magistrate, Mr Henderson the gamekeeper, and Mr Bainbridge the headmaster, with Mrs Yarrow from the post office accompanying them and making notes – had done their rounds and soon, with the tardy Mayor Graham in tow, they were doing them again. Mayor Graham was a tiny man in his sixties. When Gerry got a look at him – he and the other judges passed by the Garland, and Gerry was on her feet at once, leaning on someone's shoulder, stretching to her full height to see over the crowd, one hand shielding her eyes from the glare – she didn't know whether to be repelled or fascinated by just how incredibly tiny he was. She would be amazed if anyone could think of anything else to say about him. Ray was hardly a giant among men – he was taller than you'd think, mind, those narrow shoulders took a bit off him – but she wasn't embarrassed to Lindy Hop with him. Imagine trying to Lindy Hop with the diminutive Mayor Graham! Imagine doing anything with him. 'Look at his hands . . .' she said to nobody in particular. Also, he had an especially small mouth and very pink lips that were never still.

Gerry had returned to her seat and Jimmy had resumed telling her some interminable yarn, when she noticed that her elder daughter had decided to put in an appearance.

'And where've you been all this time?'

When Izzy replied that she had been sliding on the dance floor with the farmer's son, the men laughed as though she were joking. Gerry rolled her eyes. It was good to see that Mam was in a canny fettle because Izzy had had an excellent idea: they should buy some hens. She'd seen some for sale – lovely, golden brown birds, and tame as anything – and the man, whose name was Mr Monaghan, had even let her hold one (it was lighter than you'd think, like holding a balloon, apart from the feet which were scratchy and surprisingly warm) and he'd told her to tell her dad that they were champion layers. Getting Mam and Dad to do what she wanted, especially when it involved buying something, was not an activity with which Izzy had historically enjoyed much success, but the urgency of her desire inspired her to try. It was simply a matter of choosing the right tactics. It would still be best to try and press Dad into buying the hens first, and then the two of them could work on talking Mam round to the idea. So while Mam was chatting to someone else, Izzy started explaining how Dad would be able to sell the eggs, so that the hens would soon pay for themselves. She was careful to use this phrase more than once since a thing paying for itself was, she had noticed, often the aim of Dad's inventions. Annie, watching how Izzy was mithering Dad, caught her excitement and fell in step, agreeing wholeheartedly that it was an excellent idea to buy hens.

It had just occurred to Gerry that Mayor Graham was awarding prizes for the biggest leek, the biggest beet, and so forth, and the image of someone so small appraising a giant leek suddenly struck her as irresistibly funny. She began to emit a series of snorts, but was quite incapable of telling Ray why. Gerry's smile, bestowed unwillingly, was enchanting; her laughter less so. Ray, feeling the situation beginning to slide from him, and assuming Gerry to be laughing at this bloke's story, stood up and finished his pint at a gulp. To the delight of Izzy and Annie, he then declared his intention to go and have a look at the chickens and see what he thought of them. He motioned to Gerry that she would be coming too.

*

The climax of May Day, or so it seemed to the Whippers, was the evening's competition to determine which of the rams would be that year's tup: this – and no more than this – had been explained to them by the men in the Garland. The beasts had been penned behind the pub all day, and were on high alert, with the scent of rival rams in their nostrils. The first two contenders were led out onto the green separately by two pairs of men: the rams had been blindfolded, and fitted with heavy wooden collars with long iron handles attached, so that the men could lead them while staying clear of the horns. Slowly, the two groups neared one another, the two rams jerking and bucking, trying to shake their heads free of their blindfolds. At the centre of it all stood Jack in the Green. High above his head he held a sort of double-ended bridle. A hush descended as he lowered his arms, in time with the two rams being brought within range. With a few nimble movements he fastened either end of the bridle to the beasts' necks, drawing the ends tight as the rams were allowed to edge closer to one another. The two groups of men were now leaning back from each other, each man's heels dug into the green, so that it looked like a tug of war. The Whippers watched these proceedings in perplexed silence, and Ray and Gerry, the only adult spectators who did not know what would happen next, had the dreamy sense of being children again.

'May the hardest-headed win!' declared Jack in the Green, taking a few steps back and raising his arms as the crowd roared in approval. At a stroke, the rams were released from their wooden collars and their blindfolds were snatched away. They stood facing one another, yoked together. The handlers backed off hurriedly to a safe distance. Dazzled in the sunlight, the rams shook their heads and danced about for a few seconds, pulling at the yoke until, at once, each seemed to become more fully aware of the other, and then they each backed up a few steps until the bridle was pulled taut – and then they charged, butting heads with a ferocity that made Ray wince.

Again and again the animals reared and butted one another, finding a rhythm of their own, sometimes pausing for a few seconds as though by mutual consent, more often taking advantage of the other one's wish to rest a moment. The dull whack of impact carried in the still evening air with horrible clarity, and although Gerry had been looking away after the first butt, she found it impossible not to visualise what followed from the sound alone. It quickly became clear which of the beasts was going to be victorious, but even when the loser collapsed in a stunned heap, its front legs buckled under it, the competition kept on, and the victor was allowed to continue butting his fallen rival until Jack in the Green cried, 'Death on the horns!' and the handlers finally returned to drag the ram away from its rival.

All around Ray money changed hands while murmured verdictives and predictions were offered, making him notice retrospectively the silence that had been observed during the competition. Two men, boys really, were dragging the stunned beast by its hind legs away to the side of the green. He didn't think it was dead; he couldn't tell for sure, of course, but he thought it was just stunned. Ray seemed to break out of a trance. If he was going to leave, if he was going to take the girls away from this, he would have to act quickly – the handlers had already begun to wrestle the next two rams towards the green.

'Let's away,' he said briefly, watching himself from high above leading his family back through the crowd, trying not to make eye contact with anyone so that he didn't have to compose even a silent response to what he'd just witnessed. 'Let's away . . .' he murmured again.

It was an unpleasant surprise to discover that he had not actually made a move. To do so would in any case have been difficult, given the press of bodies around him, and where were the lasses? Were they watching this? He wanted to call for them but the great hush had descended once again. Gerry was behind him to his left; he could feel her clutching the sleeping Bairn tightly to her breast. He could imagine her clenched jaw, the little knot of anger she carried in her shoulders when she was starting to seethe but unable to give expression to it yet.

The two groups of handlers were starting to near one another again, starting to get into their tug-of-war formation, and Jack in the Green was holding the bridle aloft. Much of his green body paint was streaky with sweat now. Was it the same bloke every year, Ray wondered, or did they pick a new one? He had his part down pat in any case, slipping the bridle over the two rams' heads as though it were something he did every day.

'May the hardest-headed win!'

The hush intensified, becoming a solid element in which the crowd was held imprisoned. The handlers unfastened the wooden collars and whipped away the rams' blindfolds – but no: one of the men slipped and fell on his arse; and he'd failed to remove the blindfold properly. The ram thrashed its head wildly. A collective gasp went up as the man scrambled to his feet and reached in to tug it free. Now he was off, rejoining his fellows, safe, abashed. The other ram was still pawing the ground, unaware of the advantage it had missed, when the first ram, knowing its work when it saw it, backed up a few steps and then reared and butted. This bout did not last as long as the first.

Izzy and Annie had been shoving forwards to get a better view, and by the time they realised that they were separated from Mam and Dad, the crowd had locked into place around them. It was okay, though; they would find Mam and Dad again after, and at least they had a good view now. And so they had watched the first two bouts, held in place firmly as a pair of pegs. The movement of the beasts rearing and butting reminded Izzy of something – waves breaking over a jutting outcrop of rocks, or the threshing motion of the topmost branches of a conifer in a high wind . . . The slow, almost dignified rearing up on hind legs, the fraction of a second when both beasts hung suspended upright, and then the savage, dull thump as the heads came together. The way their back legs kicked out after they had butted each other. It had its own rhythm, a sort of stateliness that Izzy couldn't say she minded. It was, she supposed, a natural process; a winnowing, albeit in an extreme form. The competition had been intensified by yoking the beasts together, obviously, but still, this is what they were born for. And now the second winner had been discovered, and the weaker ram had been identified and – sacrificed? Izzy tried the word; it seemed to fit.

'Death on the horns!' cried Jack in the Green.

There was a break in the action now as the handlers had to

manage the difficult trick of getting the victor of the second bout, which Izzy gathered was a Northalbion Blueface, back in its wooden collar. It was like an extra competition, this, Izzy thought, only it was obvious that the men were going to win really. Unless the ram managed to stick one of them with his horns. She saw a woman nearby steal a glimpse at the men wrestling with the ram and then look away, steal a glimpse and then look away; Izzy practised doing likewise. She could hear a man behind her predicting that the Northalbion Blueface would beat the Rough Fell, he had no doubt, and another man said aye, but the Rough Fell was a big bugger and all so we'll see.

By the time the third bout got under way, with the two victors facing off against each other, Izzy had to admit that she was interested to see who the winner would be. The men didn't bother blindfolding the rams this time – was that because of the man who'd slipped and nearly spoiled things? Or did they never bother with the blindfold for the final bout, since the beasts surely knew what was coming by now? Annie's face looked like she'd tasted lemon juice or vinegar. Izzy briefly mimicked the expression, but it interfered with her vision so she let it drop. May the hardest-headed win.

The two beasts stood facing one another. They were both huge; the Blueface might have been the larger of the two. What if they broke the bridle and came charging at the crowd? If they worked together they could probably snap the bridle. Izzy wondered if that had ever happened. They were snorting like horses, and now they were backing away from each other, readying to charge. Their wool was long and raggy – Izzy couldn't imagine it ever being turned into anything you'd want to wear. Even though she was expecting it, the burst of speed when they charged took her by surprise. They connected with a hollow-sounding whack, back legs flailing out behind them almost comically, and then collected themselves and trotted back to make ready for another charge.

Their eyes were ever so placid, even though they were fighting, that was the thing. You'd never know they were angry or anything. They butted again, and again, and again . . . It was like watching a mechanism that renewed itself, two pistons firing, each one triggering the other, like one of Dad's perpetual-motion machines that you thought would keep going for ever except they never did; and now the Rough Fell was down, lying on one side, its feet twitching. But the Blueface wasn't about to let up, and charged at its fallen rival. The butting continued until the Rough Fell's skull caved like a soft fruit, a small arc of blood pelted out, and the beast lay still for good.

Izzy took Annie's hand and they pushed their way through the bodies as the crowd broke up. Neither had spoken during the ram competition, and neither of them would quite be able to find the words to talk of it later; it was obviously the sort of thing best forgotten, but here and now was a time for holding hands. Annie was having a bit cry, so Izzy was being the brave one. It took something out of the ordinary to bring them back into this sort of alignment, which is how they had once been all the time, when Annie had been very little and Izzy was still going to school.

Ray was braced for Gerry's fury at being forced to witness the business with the rams, but as they got free of the crowd at last and could face one another, he saw by her faraway look that the anger, or something like it, was still there, but would not be showing itself just yet. She did not want to discuss what had just happened; it could be that she would never mention it. He had come to be something of an expert on Gerry's inner weather. Needs must.

While the couple weighed their options the lasses rejoined them. Across the way a bonfire had been built, though the locals insisted on calling it a Baal Fire, for whatever difference that made, and Annie had been very excited at the prospect of seeing this, though she seemed subdued now; maybe she was tiring. At the same time, the dancing over at the village hall would soon be under way – a trumpet and trombone could already be heard vamping something that might be 'If You Could See Me Now' – and, though the Whippers' expectations were low, the prospect of having a dance was half the reason they had come to the fair in the first place.

It was at last decided that the children, under Izzy's supervision, would go to see the Baal Fire, while Mam and Dad went for a dance at the village hall. They would meet back at the same spot when the dancing was done with and all go home together. The Bairn, fast asleep in Gerry's arms, wrapped in his blanket like a king in hiding, was transferred, with no small amount of ceremony, to Izzy's arms. Strict instructions and meaningful looks were conveyed to Izzy by her mother at this time. Annie really was being uncharacteristically quiet, Ray thought. That done, the girls made their way over towards the already smoking Baal Fire, while the grown-ups headed for the village hall, walking briskly so as to avoid the chance of having to talk about the thing with the rams.

The village hall was bleak enough: a raftered shell of a place with a few flags draped over the worst patches of dry rot. The band had set up at the far end, looking incongruously spruce with their white jackets and brilliantined quiffs. According to the faded legend on the face of the bass drum, Fats Paul and His All-Stars was the name of the outfit. The hall began to fill, and the band got under way: with a snap of the snare drum they plunged into 'Memphis in June', segueing from that to 'The Things We Did Last Summer'. Ray and Gerry were among the first couples to dance, attracting looks, of course, but also fellow dancers.

The band was tight, better than Eshwood deserved, and Gerry approved. She soon sensed that the musicians were playing for themselves, for the love of it, for the gods, and that was always the best thing, she thought, when the band were really lost in it, and you knew the music was a better recompense than whatever fee they were due or the applause of the crowd. Can't Get Out of This Mood. Oh, this was old school, just what she wanted to hear. Sweetness. Sweetness! Gerry felt that she'd been carrying the Bairn around for days, and of course she didn't begrudge it but by God, it was good to be free. Cares slid away as she and Ray mirrored each other, barely breaking eye contact, catching and slipping each other's grasp with a fluency beyond practice. You Always Hurt the One You Love. Some of these numbers she'd've rolled her eyes at had they been played on a real dance floor, but here there was no shame, no need to feign disapproval, and the band were playing out of their skins. Fashions may have been on the turn and the Saturday-night variety shows may have been drying up, but this was the music the band had formed to play, and they were here to show everyone how. You'd Be So Nice to Come Home to. How did it ever slip her mind that Ray was the best dance partner she'd ever had? She felt them moving together as one, for all to see like a flame over oil. Where Can I Go Without You. At last they were getting into the slower numbers; Gerry was exhausted, but for all that, she felt an ache as the set began to wind down. I'm a Fool to Want You. They would *have* to dance again soon somehow. Izzy was old enough to be left in charge for an evening – Whindale wasn't a million miles away, or they could drive to Oldshield for heaven's sake, bugger the damage. She was resolved. Into Each Life Some Rain Must Fall. Full Moon and Empty Arms.

*

Outside, the lasses were watching the Baal Fire, which was now well under way. It had dried Annie's tears, and made her forget the reason for them. It had kept the Bairn asleep by warming him: he was a forgotten weight in Izzy's arms. Izzy's bright, vacant eyes were fixed on the searing heart of the fire; eventually she let her gaze drift up to take in the flames that licked and lapped at the darkness, and, high above, the rigid, brilliant stars. It was the biggest fire she'd ever seen. She couldn't believe that it wouldn't just keep growing – take root and burn for ever, maybe, or else spread to the forest and engulf all England. The enormous cracking sounds it made as it burned were like those of a monster crashing through a forest after its prey.

The children of the village stood around the fire. It seemed as though it belonged to them, there were so few adults in attendance. Izzy's cheeks were warmed by the blaze but she could feel the cool evening gathering at her neck and shoulders as the sunset melted away. Why, she wondered, did people like to watch a fire? It was next best to a living thing, and you felt involved in it by just being there and gazing at it, she thought. To watch a fire was to exist in time and to know it, to be aware of each passing moment, but pleasantly so; whereas usually you only noticed time when you were unhappy or dreading something that was going to happen. Izzy looked at the faces of the children around her; if she were going to school, some of these might be friends of hers by now, and she'd know about them, and they wouldn't just be faces; but there was no use in thinking such thoughts as these, and by the time her parents found her and Annie it was growing late, and Ray said they'd better look sharp and get away home before dark – and so, after collecting their cages of restive chickens from Mr Monaghan (in the end Ray had relented and bought seven birds), that's what they did.

5

Tell Me True

'This – *this!* – is what comes of clarting about with scruffy little beggars in the village. This is what comes of it!' Gerry explained. Izzy stood before her; she couldn't disagree. They were in the parlour, which was hardly the place to be doing this, but what choice did Gerry have? She couldn't very well do it in Ray's shed, could she? 'I take my eyes off you for five minutes. Five minutes! And you're off doing Christ knows what with Christ knows who. Take your top off, then!'

Gerry was having a wretched morning. First, Ray's latest hare-brained scheme to patent a steam-powered egg timer or whatever it was this time had been knocked back: the letter had arrived that morning, so *he* was in a terrific fettle and sharing the goodwill with everyone; and then the Bairn had been especially twisty all morning, which wasn't like him, not really, which made her think that something might be wrong, though she was probably worrying over nothing, or so she told herself; and then, of course, Lady Muck herself, Miss Claiborne, had decided that this was the day she wanted to get a look at Izzy and Annie, because Gerry didn't have enough to do already. To cap it all, she's combing Izzy's hair and trying to make her look a bit less like a street urchin, and what does she discover but that Izzy's got nits and didn't even have the sense to tell anyone. No wonder she'd been scratching her head all week like a monkey. God, was there ever such a misfortunate idiot born? No doubt she'd have just kept on scratching herself for ever if Gerry hadn't told her to pack it in. It was exhausting!

'And did you spare a thought for the Bairn? Did you think, for one sodding minute, about what it would be like if the Bairn got your disgusting nits? Christ in heaven. Christ in hell!' Gerry looked at Izzy's skinny shoulders, the clavicles, the numbered ribs. She could scream. She dipped the bristle brush in the bucket of turpentine and started scrubbing at Izzy's head. It was disgusting, that's what it was. And it stank. It was making the whole place stink. The smell of it had got the Bairn started crying and everything, she could hear him from his cot upstairs. Her hands were stinging. Her eyes were streaming. Izzy had started to bubble and cry, that was the next thing, and Annie wasn't helping matters either – did she ever! – jumping around and shout-singing:

> *Queenie, Queenie Caroline,*
> *Washed her hair with turpentine,*
> *She really thought she looked so fine*
> *Because she wore a crin-o-line!*

'You'd just better hope *you* don't have them and all,' snapped Gerry. That shut Annie's trap. 'Go and see to the Bairn, will you? Give him his bottle, for God's sake!'

This was her Saturday. This was her weekend, when other people put their feet up and relaxed. Other women would be shopping on Oldshield High Street, having their hair done and what-not. Looking back to her work, she saw that it was hopeless. The idiot's hair was heaving. Infested. She was wasting her time. Her fingers were red raw, too. Gerry took Izzy by the hair, shoved her head into the bucket and held it there. Izzy was struggling, of course, as if Gerry had got her nose and mouth under the surface, which she *hadn't*, it was just the hair and scalp. Probably the fumes were a bit much, but it wasn't for long. She just needed a good soaking. How else was she supposed to get rid of them? There was one floating off now. The turps was doing the trick. 'Hold still! I *said*, hold *still*!'

2

'My word, girl, you are thin! Look at you! Why in heaven's name are you so *thin*? And your eyes, they're positively *sunken*...' Miss Claiborne's stare was unwavering, disbelieving. She looked as though she were examining something in a cage. She always looked like that, but on this occasion she intended to.

Izzy felt marooned in the cavernous bedroom. In the

distant, tarnished mirrors her doppelgängers stood vigil. It was so embarrassing, the pitying look that grown-ups gave her, and always the same questions: didn't anybody feed her? Was there something wrong with her? Questions you weren't supposed to answer, and that made the silence after them heavy. But what could Izzy do about any of this? She would just have to stand there and endure Miss Claiborne's pity for a minute or so. Grown-ups lost interest soon enough. Even now, Miss Claiborne was sitting back in her pillows, adjusting to the situation, finding a comfortable place in it.

Izzy glanced around the room. She was standing under a vast, grey-green chandelier that made her think of seaweed; she imagined the room as the seabed, and Miss Claiborne in her four-poster bed became a puffy old fish hiding in some coral. Through the tall windows the bleak noonday light filled the room to the brim. It was more like an aquarium than the sea. In a moment, Izzy thought, she's going to ask me how old I am, and I'll tell her I'm thirteen and she won't believe me, and that's how this interview will end, thank God. But first, Miss Claiborne had something to show Izzy. She called the girl nearer. Izzy obediently shuffled a few inches closer to the bed, hoping with a passion that the old lady wouldn't notice the smell of turpentine. Izzy had an especial dread of getting embarrassed today because if that happened she would blush: she imagined her warm head growing odoriferous like a foul pomander.

From her bedside table, Miss Claiborne produced what appeared at first to be a large ball of fluff. And this was why Izzy had been summoned.

'This is what girls used to do at about this time of year when I was your age. We would make a tisty-tosty ball.' To judge by Izzy's blank expression, she'd never heard of such a thing. Well, Miss Claiborne had expected as much, given how quickly children grew up nowadays, how neglected the old ways had become in our haste-ridden world. She handed the ball to Izzy, who clearly didn't know what to do with it. 'It's made of cowslips,' said Miss Claiborne.

Izzy nodded; she could see that.

'I had young Sheila pick some for me. I wondered if I'd be able to remember how to make one – as you can see, I could!'

Izzy nodded and tried to smile, but Miss Claiborne wasn't looking at her now.

'Yes, once the warm weather had brought out the meadow flowers, Mother used to send us out, my sister Effy and I, to pick cowslips. We'd to give them to Cook to make wine. Of course, girls being girls, we'd save the prettiest blooms, and tie them all together with wool, and make a tisty-tosty ball. Then we would play Tell Me True. Do girls still play Tell Me True, I wonder?'

Izzy blinked helplessly.

'Pity. A sweet game. Each girl throws the ball in the air, and recites a little rhyme:

> *Tisty Tosty, tell me true,*
> *Who shall I be married to?*
> *Tisty Tosty, cowslip ball,*
> *At my sweetheart's name you'll fall.*

'And after that you'd recite as many boys' names as you could think of, throwing and catching the ball as you did so, and when you missed your catch or dropped the ball, well, that was the name of the boy you were going to marry.'

Izzy looked at the weightless ball of fluff. She had not, to the best of her knowledge, given the subject of marriage, or indeed the subject of boys, a moment's thought. What would she do if Miss Claiborne demanded that she play a round of Tell Me True? Right at this moment, the only boy's name she could think of was 'Nodge', and that wasn't even a real name. She pictured herself throwing the ball in the air, saying, 'Nodge, Nodge, Nodge . . .'. She very much hoped Miss Claiborne was not about to ask her to do this.

'It was nonsense, of course,' said Miss Claiborne complacently. 'One would make sure to drop the tisty-tosty ball when the name of the boy one had taken a fancy to was mentioned. In consequence it appeared deeply meaningful.'

Izzy thought, this room is the heart of the Hall, and Miss Claiborne is the shard of ice in the heart.

Miss Claiborne became once more aware that Izzy was standing before her, and gave her a thin, forbearing smile.

'I suppose we were silly girls. You must think we were deeply silly girls!'

Izzy quickly assured her that no, she didn't think this.

There was a moment of silence, and then Miss Claiborne remembered something. 'And how old are you?' she asked.

Gerry was hanging about, waiting for the old girl to finish with Izzy, then she might be able to sit down for five minutes. It wasn't a bad day. She found herself looking idly at Hobbs, who was across the way setting out pea sticks or something. Squinting in the sun gave him an expression of merry contempt for the world that made so few demands on him.

'Busy day?' asked Gerry, walking over.

Hobbs looked at the ground and looked at his hands and said that once he was done here he'd earth up the potatoes. Gerry couldn't help but notice that he hadn't tried to make his answer any more interesting on her behalf. Perhaps that piqued her. In any case, she tried again.

'At least the weather's holding up.'

Hobbs relented, and asked how they were liking life at Eshwood Hall.

'We're settling in. It's certainly a change from our last place at Ubbansford. That was a poky little place we had, on the pit rows, you know. It had a dirt floor! In this day and age. Can you believe. That's where Ray was working, down the pit at Butterlaw. Always plenty of folk to have a bit chat with, though. I will say that for it. You feel like you're a thousand miles from anywhere out here.'

'You've moved about quite a bit, according to your Izzy.'

'Oh, yes. We started out with nowt, and we've still got most of it left, as they say. Izzy was born in a Nissen hut! So I suppose we've gone up in the world since then . . .'

Gerry asked Hobbs for a cigarette but he said he didn't

have any, and remarked that Izzy seemed like a nice lassie, and that she had quite an imagination on her.

'Oh, she has the imagination, all right. Drives me up the wall at times. She once told little Annie that she was adopted. I bet she hasn't mentioned that to you. It's true: I leave them alone for five minutes while I have a lie-down: five minutes! And she can't get Annie to behave or something, so she tells her that she's adopted. And when that doesn't have the desired effect, she tells her that actually the fairies left her on the doorstep, and nobody else wanted her, so she'd better behave, or else Izzy'd give her back to the bloody fairies. Next thing I know Annie's screaming and crying that the fairies are coming to take her away.'

Hobbs laughed politely, and offered to keep the lasses entertained, if ever they were bored, by getting them to help pick the radishes and baby turnips and that. Then Gerry felt a stone in her shoe and, leaning on his shoulder for balance, slipped it off and gave it a shake.

Just then Izzy, released from her interview with Miss Claiborne, came over to join them, and the familiar greeting she gave Hobbs prompted Gerry to observe that the two must have already met, as if she had just surmised this.

'Oh, yes,' said Izzy. 'Sam's the gardener. He's the one who told us about the Grey Lady. He's seen her and everything.' Gerry gave Hobbs a look that made him shift his weight. Izzy took this to mean that her mam didn't believe her – but, as it was true, she pushed the point: 'Tell her! And I bet you've seen other ghosts and all.'

Hobbs tried to laugh this off, but Gerry assured him that

she'd love to hear about the ghosts that had been keeping Izzy up all night since they moved in.

'Well,' he said, rubbing his chin, 'I did see a *phantam* once . . .'

Izzy bobbed on her toes in delight, and asked him what he did when he saw it.

'Well, I shot it! And I et it for tea!' And then, as neither Gerry nor Izzy seemed to get the joke, he explained sheepishly that a phantam, with an 'a' instead of an 'o', was a cross between a cock pheasant and a hen bantam.

'Yes, well, at this rate our girls will end up in the cooking pot as well. It's been a week and we're yet to get an egg out of them.'

'They're not gan to clock yet, eh?' said Hobbs amiably.

Gerry stared at him uncomprehendingly, but refused to ask for a translation. After a moment she remarked again that, yes, the chickens would end up going to the butcher at this rate, and with that, she left them.

Hobbs took up his hoe and fell to weeding the driveway, and then said more quietly to Izzy,

'Now, listen, Izzy: you'd best keep out of them woods. We don't want you getting yourself lost in there.'

'Who says I've been in the woods?'

Hobbs gave her an old-fashioned look, but didn't reply.

Izzy asked if the woods were haunted. It would be fun to hear another ghost story – maybe the Grey Lady went walking there at midnight! Izzy pictured a winter night, and a cowled form flitting between wick-black tree trunks, ephemeral and floaty as egg-white in water . . .

Hobbs grinned at her question, and then stopped

grinning, and then straightened up and said, '*Haunted*. Well, I cannot say the woods *is* haunted, and I cannot say they're *isn't*. But I'll tell you one thing: there's seven bairns buried in them woods, and we don't need an eighth!'

Izzy's eyes were like saucers. 'Who buried the bairns?'

'Well, the Claibornes did. That's to say, it's their bairns what's buried there. Aye, all seven of Miss Claiborne's young brothers and sisters. They all died when they were just little, you see. That's how things was, back in the day. Bairns got sick and died over the least bit thing, and you just had to allow it as nature's way.'

Izzy thought back to her walks in the woods. She'd had no idea that she might at any moment have stumbled upon the graves of seven bairns. Seven! 'I did go for a walk in the woods,' Izzy admitted, 'but I didn't get lost . . .' She told herself that this was only half-untrue, since, although she had become lost for a *while*, she had subsequently found her way home, so had not *really* been lost at all, as it turned out.

Hobbs turned to face her. 'What's a young lassie like you want with tramping about in the woods, anyways?'

In reply, Izzy surprised herself by telling him about the Chapel, and the wooden throne, though she didn't describe the visions she'd had the first time she sat in it. But she did tell him how much she liked visiting the place. He could, of course, tell on her to Mam and Dad, and then they could, of course, see to it that she didn't get to go back to the Chapel, but somehow she felt Hobbs was on her side, and would keep this confidence. He was impressed enough by her story to pause in his work, and rest his weight on his hoe.

'So you found your way to the Chapel,' mused Hobbs, 'and you liked what you saw . . .' He tried to weigh the situation up. He didn't want this lassie getting lost in the woods, but it should be said here that the man had no children of his own; he had no nieces or nephews. He wouldn't have been able to guess Izzy's age, and knew nothing whatever of childish ways or proper bedtimes. And all of this happened long ago, when such matters were thought of far less than they are now. So he trusted that this girl's parents would see to her safety. And if she was curious, where was the harm in talking of local history and such?

So it was that Izzy learned all about the Chapel and how it dated back at least as far as the thirteenth century, making it much older than Eshwood Hall. Nobody knew why anyone had seen fit to build a church just there, slap bang in the middle of the woods, but there it was. Back in those days, you might have a dream in which an angel or what-have-you instructed you to build a church, so you built one: that's how most churches got to be where they are now. It had been deconsecrated in the last century, though some might speculate as to how consecrated it had ever really been. The carvings on the walls and the ceiling inside were of great interest to the scholars, and Hobbs knew of at least two visits from university men, one from Unthank College and one from the University of Oldshield, who had come up especially just to look at the carvings and draw them and make notes on them, and their findings had probably later been published.

'Who are the men on the ceiling, the ones with leaves

growing out of their faces?' asked Izzy, since Hobbs didn't seem about to volunteer this information.

'Ah, that's the Green Man.'

'There was loads of them. Green *men*,' corrected Izzy.

'There's only the one Green Man. He just takes different shapes as it suits him. So some folk say he looks a bit like this, and some folk say he looks a bit like that.'

'What does he do?'

'Do? Well, he . . . he does as he pleases, I reckon. He presides over his domain,' Hobbs declared expansively. And then he struck upon an idea: 'He keeps nosy parkers out of the woods: he chases them out! And he looks after the woods and the wild creatures and that, and makes sure the seasons get turned round on time, and what-have-you. He's been here for ever, all over England, long before anyone'd even thought to call it "England".'

Izzy speculated that perhaps the Green Man had himself been the one who first called the place England, and Hobbs concurred that this was as likely as anything else to be the case. And then, since both parties felt they had strayed a little beyond their areas of expertise, and a little beyond their usual vocabularies, they talked about the henhouse that Izzy had helped her dad to make, which was excellent and made of wood and wire and had a ramp and nesting boxes and everything, and was quite big really because it had to fit seven hens inside.

'Seven hens and no cockerel . . .' Hobbs marvelled. 'They'll be tearing strips off each other!'

4

Annie looks at the carpet which is purple and thick and has got rugs on it which is daft because you don't need rugs when you've got a carpet. The carpet's so thick Annie feels like she's standing on a huge cake. She looks up and Miss Claiborne's looking at her. Miss Claiborne asks again if Annie wants to hear about India. She's got loads of old letters around her where she's sitting up in bed. Annie can smell the old letters and they smell musty. What's India Annie asks and Miss Claiborne says why it's a place it's a colony come child you must know that. Annie looks out the window at the treetops. The treetops are dead still. Two birds fly up far away and Annie watches them until they disappear. Miss Claiborne says Uncle Freddie was in India and his letters were most amusing and were written with dash. Uncle Freddie was dashing. His letters were always jaunty as letters should essentially be and when he came back the stories he could tell made everybody laugh ever so much because he could do the voices. Annie looks up at the chandelier and it's massive and a funny colour. Miss Claiborne is turning over an envelope slowly and says Cousin Henry was in India as well of course. Annie asks if Cousin Henry's letters were jaunty and Miss Claiborne says no they were not they were dull because Cousin Henry was morbid. What's morbid mean asks Annie and Miss Claiborne says dull. Now Annie feels sorry for Cousin Henry for being morbid. They were full of criticism says Miss Claiborne meaning the letters. Cousin Henry didn't much want to be in India and he didn't seem to much want anyone else to be over there either. Annie looks at the panelling and wonders if there's a secret compartment. There's probably a secret opening somewhere but you have to know how to open it and Miss Claiborne doesn't know about it because that's who it's kept secret from. Once you're inside the walls you can go anywhere in the Hall and it's excellent. Miss Claiborne says she's deciding which letters to keep and which ones to burn. She's going to burn the ones that she doesn't want any more and that she doesn't want other people to read. Are you going to make a Baal Fire like on May Day Annie asks but Miss Claiborne says she doesn't have enough letters for that so she'll just burn them in the fire there in the room. Annie wants to see the letters burning but Miss Claiborne says she has to listen to her reading from them first. Annie can smell the letters and she can smell dried flowers or it might be perfume that smells like dry flowers. She looks at Miss Claiborne and thinks how everything Miss Claiborne does is dead slow. It must take her half an hour to eat a bun. Annie looks out the window and there's another bird flying along the sky. Now Miss Claiborne has found a letter she wants to read out and she reads it out but she keeps skipping over bits that Annie wouldn't appreciate and interrupting the letter to say things about the people in the letter. It goes on for ages and Miss Claiborne says she's deciding which letters to keep as she goes along. She's putting the ones she wants to keep in a dispatch case where they'll be safe. It takes ages but eventually she's decided and has finished reading bits out and Annie has been behaving herself and now it's time to take the letters from Miss Claiborne and that means she has to go right up to her and she doesn't like going right up to her. Annie's scared but Mam's told her if she starts crying or screaming when she's in there with Lady Muck she'll get an absolute hiding when she gets back. Annie takes a handful of letters which are dead dry and weigh hardly anything like dry leaves. She takes them over to the fire and chucks them on but Miss Claiborne says not to do it like that for heaven's sake or she'll put the fire out or fill the room with smoke. She has to feed them into the fire a few at a time. But it's okay because the fire's not gone out and after a few minutes the letters are burning. Annie's right in front of the fire and can feel it prickling her cheeks and making her eyes sting a bit. Annie goes back to Miss Claiborne who gives her some more letters and says now feed them in a few at a time. So that's what Annie does she feeds them in a few at a time. They burn Cousin Henry's letters first. Annie enjoys watching them darken and curl up like fists.

5

Izzy stared up at the moon. It wasn't bath day until tomorrow, but she'd secretly taken herself down to the burn before bed, and had scrubbed copious amounts of Imperial Leather into her hair and washed it until the strands squeaked between her fingers; somehow it still smelled faintly of turpentine.

Her scalp felt like it had shrunk tight around her skull like a dried-up lemon. She propped herself on one elbow and peered out into the darkness.

A moon made all the difference, and on a clear night like this you could see surprisingly well once your eyes had adjusted. Dad's work-shed was there, and the dilapidated orangery . . . She hadn't been looking more than a minute when she saw, stepping out from the darkness of the woods, a mother roe and her fawn: silent as a pair of ghosts on tiptoe they came, the mother taking the lead, the fawn staying close. They moved into the moonlight as you might move across the stage in an empty theatre, and proceeded to inspect Ray's work-shed, sniffing at the pots of paint and what-have-you, and all but disappearing inside until only their white scuts were visible in the gloom. Now they reappeared, the mother first – watchful, suspicious – and the fawn following on. Izzy could almost feel the strength of the trust that bonded them as they moved on their delicate, springing heels across the driveway, and began to melt once more into the shadows of the trees.

When the scratching sounds began, Izzy was able to tell herself that she was just imagining them, that they were nothing but an echo of her itchy, fizzing scalp; but soon the noises grew louder, fiercer – whatever was making them would not be denied. The roe were out of sight now, and Izzy turned back in her bed and gave herself unhappily to a study of the noises. At least they weren't in the room with her this time: she could tell that on this occasion the noises were certainly coming from downstairs.

Abruptly, the scratching and the whispering ceased, and after a few seconds of pregnant silence, another sound reached her: breaking crockery – or no, breaking *china*. The whip of air as it was whisked from the Welsh dresser, the crash of its impact on the flagstones, the grinding as it was crushed to dust. Izzy began to count how many times this sound occurred: four . . . five . . . To this was added the shunt and squeal of the sofa being punted and dragged across the floor – and that must be Mam's chair, the chesterfield, rolling like a huge die inside a room-sized Ludo cup.

Izzy, who was now sitting up in bed with her back to the headboard and her knees tucked under her chin and the sheets gathered around her, which is the safest way to be in a bed, looked over at Annie, who was – impossibly! – sleeping peacefully. And in the next room, of course, the Bairn must also be dreaming undisturbed, though that was less surprising – he could sleep through anything when he was in the mood. Izzy was alone with the ghosts, wide-eyed in the dark, grinding her teeth to stop them chattering. How long this ordeal lasted she could not say, but as suddenly as the racket had begun, it ended: night-time silence washed back into the house, broken only by the gentle snores of her dad next door, and her clamorous heartbeat pounding for her ears alone.

6

The Green Man

I

To be fair, Ray was already having a rare morning. First, his repairs to the pipes in Miss Claiborne's bathroom had come undone during the night and now it was raining in the library. Was he a plumber? No, he was not. Had he ever claimed to be a plumber? No. He had not. He was a chauffeur and odd-job man, in that order, and he could only do his best. The pipework was ancient in any case, and probably the whole lot should be ripped out and replaced, but Miss Claiborne certainly didn't want to hear anything about *that*. Eventually, after making a series of unhelpful suggestions, she had observed that Ray seemed better cut out for teaching than he was for learning – a gratuitous comment that, had he been so minded, Ray might have taken as a compliment, since it revealed that Miss Claiborne was still thinking of his connection to Sandhurst. But Ray wasn't so minded, and he cut a sorry figure as he trudged along the corridors of Eshwood Hall, back to his rooms trailing a foul mood with him, only to find Gerry (and he heard her, of course, before he saw her) up in arms screaming – like a kettle, like a madwoman, like a banshee – screaming at the lasses about something or other. He hung back in the doorway, unseen, sullen, already angrier than he could have easily admitted, trying to assess what had caused the palaver this time.

'My precious – priceless – ornaments! The few things I had! Christ in hell! Can I not leave *anything* unattended? For a second? Can't I trust you with anything? Jesus!'

Had one of the lasses broken one of Gerry's ornaments? Ray inwardly groaned at the thought of it – the breadth and the depth and the weight of Gerry's feelings, pressing down on him for hours on end . . . All would be spoiled for a day and a night at least. Since it was past help already, he held back a moment longer, watching his wife's lithe body turning, its angles – elbows, ankles – familiar from watching her dance, he supposed; her hips, which were broader than you'd think, and which any man might like to imagine holding; the colour in her cheeks; how her red hair swung . . . She was incensed.

Gerry spun round, eyes blazing, and snatched at Izzy. 'You little chit! Standing there looking guilty! It's written all over your face! It was *you*!'

'*What* was me? I didn't do anything!' Izzy protested, but she could tell her mam wasn't listening.

'Mam . . .' said Annie.

'Christ, girl, you haven't the sense to lie. I can *see* it. It was you! You smashed them to smithereens!'

'I didn't smash anything. I didn't do anything! I swear to God—'

'Mam . . .' said Annie.

'When your dad gets home he'll give you such a hiding!'

'But I don't want a hiding! Mam! Listen, I didn't *do* anything!'

'Mam . . .' said Annie.

'He'll cut the arse off you! I swear to *Christ* he will!'

Ray took this as his cue, and entered the room, asking what on earth was going on.

'Mam! I swear to God I didn't—'

'These are all I had to call my own. All I had! Except for the Bairn and – ha! – two lasses who are *worse than useless*. Worse! Jesus please us!'

'It was the ghost . . .'

Redoubtable she may have been, but these words stopped Gerry dead. Ray, who thought he'd tried everything under the sun to snap Gerry out of a rage, was almost impressed. He waited for his wife to give him his cue. When she could speak, Gerry asked Izzy to repeat herself.

'It was the *ghost*. The Grey Lady, I think. I heard it – heard her – last night, moving things about, like I've heard her every month or so since we moved in. She comes out every time there's a full moon. It's *true*. She's getting stronger – getting braver – every time. And she just wants to cause bother and that. And last night, when I couldn't sleep, I was watching the moon, and I heard . . . I heard it smashing your dolls—'

'They're not *dolls*, you *stu*pid little brat, they're *ornaments*. They're *worth* something!' Gerry's voice had a trick of shrieking on certain syllables so they seemed to thrill into Izzy's brain. Izzy felt like she was standing before a great window while a hurricane raged outside; she was watching the glass flex like a lens, not at all certain that it would hold out much longer.

Ray raised his arms and tried again to assert himself on the scene, but couldn't think of what to say other than to ask what the hell was going on.

'Mam . . .' said Annie.

'The imbecile has broken my dolls – ornaments! – and now she's lying and won't admit it. Do I need to tell you what to do? Do I need to tell you how to be a man? You should give her a bloody hiding!'

Ray's face darkened. There were things about Gerry, ways she had of talking to him, making him feel small, that he would never understand. He stored away moments such as this, intending to return and discuss them later, but once things were back on an even keel, he was always too relieved to rake back over disagreeable issues. He left the room, dragging Izzy by the wrist. Surprising though it may be, Izzy screamed for help from her mother as this happened.

Minutes later, Sheila, whose parlour was next door to the Whippers' and who had, truth to tell, paused in her knitting so as to more easily discern what all the fuss was about, heard from further off – up another floor, she presumed – the undulating wail of a child, broken by evenly paced shrieks as the blows fell. So, Sheila thought, Ray wasn't a complete drip after all.

Back in the parlour, Annie's ears were ringing. She looked at her mam. Her mam had one hand on her hip and one hand on the sideboard where her remaining dolls were still arranged. She was standing in the smithereens of the destroyed dolls. Annie judged this to be definitely the best moment to say what she had been wanting to say, so she said it.

'Mam, the Empingham Horse Fair's three weeks off, do you think Dad'll take us this year?'

2

It was later that day, that afternoon, and Izzy had been walking in the woods for some time, following a sort of path, or letting herself be led by the idea of a path. She was not thinking of the beating she had just endured, nor would she ever think of it. It was a knack she had: she could just parcel up bad memories and store them away in a far corner of her mind. She could let them gather dust.

A river makes sounds that have never been recorded, she thought, especially a fast, rocky river like the Esh. Yes, there was the sparkling, tinkling surface tinsel – and that was all most people ever heard, if they ever even listened. But there were deeper, booming, rumbling sounds forever struggling to the surface as well; things far down being turned over and over, mulled and moiled in endless confusion, as though the river were playing for time, holding back something dark among the tangleweeds and the zigzag fry.

We will never know where this train of thought might have led, for Izzy was just then distracted by an unfamiliar bird's call. It was an insistent shrill, like that of a wren but with more body to it. Holding herself still, Izzy scanned the river's surface until she saw it: a dipper! It was a thing to see a dipper, plumped and roundy, like a paperweight left on a rock by the careless river. And now – flick! – it disappeared. Izzy kept watching, waiting for the reappearance, but no, she'd missed it, because suddenly there it was already on a neighbouring rock shaking its head at her. And again – flick! – and it was gone. This time, after a few seconds, she saw it pop back out of the water, and shake its head again. For five minutes, she stayed as still as could be, watching the dipper making his rounds, completing his slow tour of his environs, in and out of the Esh . . . She tried to picture him walking on the riverbed, but it was too strange to think of a bird doing that. What must the fish make of it? And did he explore the whole length of river, or did he patrol his little patch?

At last she recommenced her moseying, and in time the path led her away from the river and deeper into the woods. She really had no idea how far she had wandered when abruptly she came to a stop at what must have been the heart of the forest, it was so dim. Izzy peered into the darkness.

The sounds seemed to be hushing or receding; something more near was coming into focus. One by one, and two by two, leaves quivered and slid, spreading and opening out onto deeper darknesses, gathering into knots of filigree. Izzy found that she was holding her breath. Branches twirled and unfurled on the edge of visibility, berries black as beetles clumped and clustered, knot holes in tree trunks widened and grew more important until they were revealed to be eye sockets, nostrils, a yawning mouth – and this was a man, this was the Green Man himself, and even as he drew himself together before her, stretching out and finding his length with a variety of creaks and crackles, Izzy knew that he had been here all along, in some form or other, watching. At last he was complete, and stood before her, seven feet tall or more, swaying gently, smoothing down some errant twigs and moss tufts behind his ears.

The Green Man's voice was deep and dry and slow, and seemed to bypass Izzy's ears altogether, softly detonating its meaning straight into her mind: *How . . . long . . . was I sleeping?*

'I . . . I don't know, I just got here,' said Izzy, for this was true.

The Green Man turned to her, as though he hadn't known she was there, and hadn't been expecting a reply. Izzy could hear his various woods articulating when he moved. His facial features were difficult to make out, as they seemed to be formed around a mistle thrush's nest, and the tangle of twigs – and the fact that the thrush was still *in* the nest – made his true expression impossible to determine. She supposed that she should have been afraid, but she didn't feel that; she felt, insofar as she could have given a name to her feelings at that precise moment, relieved to see him, as though she had been waiting for him a long time.

After a pause, he asked, *And . . . who are you?*

'I'm Izzy. Isabella.'

Isabella . . . said the Green Man thoughtfully, as he found a log, considered it, shrank a little, and then sat down with all of the slowness and ceremony that he might have employed to sit upon a throne.

The Green Man, Izzy noticed, didn't exist as a freestanding figure, and he didn't move so much as shift from one place to another like a wave on the sea, with any convenient clumps of leaves and branches gathering and reconfiguring him in the new place, just as they dispersed into their original random configurations in the place he had just left. At any one time, he might have been a trick of the light, his form dependent on looking at a scene just so. To anyone watching, Izzy would have looked like she was talking to nothing but the trees.

Isabella . . . Whipper . . . said the Green Man.

Izzy started at this: 'How did you know my name? I didn't tell you my last name.'

I know . . . all about you.

Izzy didn't see how he could know anything about her, and decided to test him. 'How old am I?'

The Green Man narrowed his eyes at her, and considered the matter. *You're as old as your tongue . . . and a little older than your teeth . . .*

Izzy rolled her eyes. She'd have to be more cunning with her questions. 'What do I want to be when I grow up?'

Why, a woman, surely . . .

'Tell me – *exactly* – something *only I* could have seen in the woods today.'

Why, your shadow . . . on a tree . . . that had been watered with last year's snow.

'All of your answers are crooked!' Izzy cried, but she was smiling.

And every time you open your mouth you say something, said the Green Man, and he was smiling too. *But why . . . did you wake me, Isabella Whipper?*

Izzy didn't have an answer for this. She certainly hadn't intended to wake him. She hadn't even known that he was sleeping; but that was the thing about waking someone, you got wrong even if you woke them accidentally. Mam always gave you wrong if you woke her up. Izzy had to give some sort of an answer, and she heard herself say that she had woken the Green Man because she needed his help. This produced a strange response: his eyes narrowed, and he stretched himself so that he was sitting more fully upright, an action accompanied by a great deal of painful-sounding creaking and ticking. This done, he asked what sort of help it was Izzy needed, so she told him about the ghost she'd been hearing, the Grey Lady as she supposed, and how scary the noises she made were, and how she seemed to be growing stronger or bolder as time went on, and how she had smashed her mam's expensive dolls and how she, Izzy, had got wrong for it.

The Green Man sighed a sigh that was the sound of dry leaves and acorn husks blown about in a hollow tree trunk. *This . . . does not sound like a ghost to me . . . It sounds . . . like a boggil.*

'A boggil!' Izzy breathed.

Yes, a boggil . . . And now that it has found you . . . I'm sorry to say . . . it will never let go of you . . . and even should you move house . . . as you Whippers so often do . . . the boggil will dog you . . . all the days of your life . . .

'But . . . what's a boggil?'

A boggil . . . is a little rattle-scawp . . . It means no one any good . . . It lives only for mischief now . . . It was a brownie, once . . . A happy, helpful creature, washing dishes, sharpening tools, darning socks and such . . . All while its hosts lay sleeping . . . So happy, so helpful, once . . . But now, from man's ingratitude, it has grown wild . . . No good can ever come of it . . .

'But *you* can get rid of it, can't you? I bet you can!'

I . . . can do what I can do . . .

'So you *can* get rid of it?'

. . . Aye . . .

Something in the Green Man's tone as he said this gave Izzy pause. '*How* are you going to get rid of it, exactly?'

I will . . . eat it . . . alive . . .

'Do you have to? Won't that, I don't know, make a mess?' Izzy had started to feel sorry for the boggil, which was ridiculous, but still.

With boggils . . . you have to make sure . . . that they're really dead . . .

'But isn't there any other way?'

The Green Man shrugged. *Perhaps . . . I could just eat the head and . . . tear up the other bits?*

'Couldn't you, I don't know, just scare him away or something?'

At this, the Green Man tumbled down flat like a house of cards, scurrying back into his constituent roots and branches. For a moment, Izzy thought that she had insulted him with her suggestion, and that he had simply deserted her; but now, to her intense relief, the ground by her feet began to stir, and up he sprang in a new configuration, no taller than a man this time, and with a face more fully formed with scraps of birch bark, which made him look older and kindlier.

Scare the boggil away . . . The Green Man mused for a long moment on this novel idea, regarding Izzy the while. *I suppose . . . I could try . . .*

'Yes, just scare it off. Just frighten it away, and that'll solve everything,' said Izzy encouragingly.

But . . . you must see to it . . . that our boggil does not return . . . for the little pests . . . do not give up their hosts easily, Isabella Whipper . . .

And so it was they made their plan: the boggil would not return until the night of the next full moon, a month from now, and that was the night the Green Man would scare it away. It would be close to the summer solstice, so the boggil's powers would be low. To ensure that it could never return to Eshwood Hall, Izzy would need to remember to wake early on Midsummer's Eve, and go out to pick herbs while the dew was still on them. The herbs of St John would be what she'd be looking for: St John's wort, mugwort, ivy, vervain, corn marigold, dwarf elder and yarrow. Any or all of those would do. She would take them and make them into a garland, and hang this from the door of the Hall, though it would have to be the servants' entrance or she'd get wrong, and that way no boggil – nor impish sprite, nor spritely imp, nor any other horrible thing – would be able to cross the threshold again.

Izzy agreed eagerly to her part of the plan. It sounded easy enough.

But . . . should I rid you of this pest . . . then you must rid me of another . . . The hammer suffers as much as the nail . . . One hand washes the other . . .

'You want *me* to do something for *you*?' Izzy couldn't think of anything she might do that would be of the least use to the Green Man.

Aye . . . a bargain must be struck . . .

Izzy waited patiently to hear the terms. After a long pause in which she became convinced that the Green Man had in fact gone back to asleep, he murmured in a confidential tone, *My woods are . . . infested . . . with rats . . . Rid me of rats . . . in payment for me . . . evicting your boggil . . .*

Izzy had already given him her promise before she realised that, really, she had no idea how to go about killing one rat, let alone an infestation. And how many rats constituted an infestation? When she'd had head lice, Mam had said she was infested – would it be like that? When she asked the Green Man for his advice, he recommended the use of gin traps, which had worked in the old days and would surely work still, and which could be found in the cellar of

Eshwood Hall. All Izzy had to do was to look behind an old press that she'd find in the furthest north-east corner of the cellar: seven iron gins would be there, each with a stake and a chain, and if she were to brush the worst of the rust from them, they would surely prove serviceable. Seven gins would catch seven rats, and the vermin would need to be dealt with after that – but that, in the Green Man's phrase, would be 'quick work, stick work or poker work', and that would be good enough by way of repayment. And so it was agreed.

3

Annie notices that most of the men are wearing hats. Some wear a flat cap and some wear a floppy black sun hat like what a scarecrow wears or a snowman. Dad tells Annie what a trilby is so she'll know one when she sees one. The best bit's the flash. They're on Fair Hill near Salt Tip Corner and there's men riding horses bareback and the horses are cantering and tossing their heads and that's the flash. Outside the Hare and Hounds there's an old man with no teeth wearing a polka-dot hankie round his neck and Annie thinks he looks right funny and tells Dad and he says aye. Most of it's good but some things are boring like some caravans are proper painted wooden wagons but most are just boring caravans. The proper painted wagons are called vardos Dad says and Annie says she wouldn't mind living in a vardo. There's little campfires and there's people sitting round the fires and some are young and some are old and wear right old coats tied with string. Annie asks Dad if they're tinkers and he says aye whisht. Sometimes on the flash the man isn't on the horse he's behind it getting pulled along in a buggy and sometimes the man just runs alongside the horse and he's holding its bridle but in any case they're flashing the horses. Annie asks Dad for a cob again but he says for God's sake will you stop mithering on about it so Annie doesn't ask him again for a bit. There's a sweetie stall and Annie asks for a poke of bullets and Dad gets her a poke of bullets. There's a man shoeing a horse and it looks cruel but Dad says it's not cruel stop your bawling. He's crouched over facing the other way and he's got the horse's back hoof up backwards over his knee and he's filing it and another man's got the horse by the bridle to keep it still while the other man's filing it. The horse doesn't know what's going on. Annie says what they're doing's cruel but Dad says it'd be cruel not to. There's some stalls selling stirrups and some stirrups are small and some's bigger and there's bridles for sale and all and Annie asks Dad if she can't get a cob can she at least get a bridle or some stirrups but Dad says what's the use of a bridle without a bloody horse. The stirrups and that are shining in the sun. Other stalls is selling leather handbags and Dad looks at them for absolutely ages because he's trying to think what to get for Mam to keep her sweet. Exmoor ponies are very small and look furry so you totally want to stroke them and give them a cuddle but they're bad-tempered because that's why they're called ex-moor ponies because they've been going absolutely wild on the moors until the farmers round them up and put them in big wagons and bring them here to sell. The Exmoor ponies go from the big wagon to the stalls over a slippery ramp that they skid about on and that just makes them more mad but once they're in the stalls they can have a sniff at the other horses in the stalls and they like that so they're happy there. There's lots of hay and that in the stalls that keeps the ponies happy and they're eating the hay. There's a man dabbing a painted number on each pony's bum once they're in the stall with a number on the end of a stick that's been dipped in paint so everyone knows whose pony's whose. Annie's with her dad trying to see the ponies in the stalls but people keep dunching into her so Dad lifts her on his shoulders and now she's got a right good view of the ponies and the horses and she's never seen that many in her entire life. There's loads of ponies all huddled together in the stalls and loads more tied up over by the Grapes. Now a man rings a handbell and Dad says the sales has started so they mosey on over towards the pen where the ponies is going up for sale and Annie's still on Dad's shoulders and it's great. There's loads of horses everywhere and you can smell them. There's a circle and it's the pen and that's where the pony goes when it's its turn and it's for sale and there's a man in the pen with a long thin stick and he taps it on the pony's bum to keep it moving around the circle though he doesn't really need to because the pony's moving anyway and the circle's so small there's nowhere for it to go except round in a circle so everyone can see it and when Dad starts hitting Izzy it's horrible and listen to her screaming blue murder Mam says but she can't help it Annie says. They're not that close but Annie's up a height on Dad's shoulders so it's fine. There's an auctioneer and Annie says is that a trilby and Dad says aye and the auctioneer's standing in a dead femmor hut that Dad says was probably just put up for the occasion and there's a sign and Annie only knows the first word which is no so she asks Dad what the sign says and he says it says no cheques accepted and she asks Dad what a cheque is and it's a drawing of some money. Is that a trilby she says and Dad says no. Is that a trilby she says and Dad says whisht Annie. Now it's the auction and it goes like this. A pony goes for £3 because it's a sucker. A pony goes for £7. A pony goes for £7 6s. A pony goes for £9. A pony goes for £7. A pony goes for £4 6s and it's a sucker as well. A pony goes for £7 and then another pony goes for £7. A pony goes for £8. Annie keeps thinking Dad's going to buy a pony but he doesn't. Annie completely wants Dad to buy a pony but he's not. There's a woman wearing a leopard headscarf and a tweed jacket and she's got bright red lipstick but it's nearly over now and she's not bought a pony. There's another woman who isn't wearing a hat but has got a fur coat and she's not bought a pony either but later Dad says it's fake fur. There's a girl standing right on the fence of the pen and she's got on a bright red duster coat with three big buttons down the front and a matching hat and she's leaning over and she's touching the ponies when they go past her but Annie can't because she's miles away. Another good bit's when they take the horses down to the Sands to get washed and the horses are plodging and splashing and it's right funny. Some policemen wear tall hats and some wear flat hats and if anything's wrong you have to tell them.

4

The horse – a gelding of uncertain age – that Ray had eventually bought at Empingham Fair cost him, after a not-inconsiderable amount of haggling, £4 5s, which was 5s more than he'd told himself he was willing to pay, and at least £1 more than it was worth. Only after the deal had been struck had it become clear to the seller (who would have accepted less) that Ray had no means of transporting the horse the twenty-odd miles back to Eshwood. Delivery was therefore arranged, for an additional fee. This was accomplished six days later, the poor beast looking even more bedraggled upon his arrival at Eshwood Hall that Monday morning.

Monday was wash day. Izzy had already scrubbed and rinsed the clothes, and now that it was warm enough to keep the mangle outside she had been there to see the wagon pulling up. Annie had been on high alert all morning, and had started to squeal with excitement as soon as she heard the engine. It's only fair to say that her excitement abated, just a little, after she got to see her new pet again, and compare its actual appearance to her memory of it. The beast was duly tied up behind Ray's work-shed; Ray would have to ask Miss Claiborne as to whether it might be kept in the stable block.

When she'd first heard about the purchase of the horse, Gerry had taken the news hard, and her shrieking had, if anything, intensified after she realised that Ray was trying to give her a new handbag – an ugly, mushroom-coloured item that wouldn't go with a thing – as a peace offering. Not having been taken to Empingham Fair in the first place, Izzy was reasonably certain that she couldn't be blamed for any of this, but she'd done her best to keep out of the way that day to be on the safe side, and had been glad to get to bed without catching hell for something or other. As far as possible, she'd kept out of the way on the day of the horse's arrival as well.

Now, idly, sleepily, Izzy watched the treeline across the driveway where the shadows were deepest, waiting to see if her eyes could adjust any more and allow her to see any further into the trees . . . The days were so long now it hardly got dark, and a full moon would pick out every eerie detail as vivid as a dream. The moon, Izzy thought, would gaze down on her, and on Eshwood village, and on all of Northalbion and everywhere, all night without blinking. It was like a salute that no one knew how to return.

*

The darkness was deepening; as Izzy stared at it she thought it was almost burning – something was shifting and writhing in the depths of the trees, making the centre of the dark enlarge like a pupil – and even now a shape began to stretch itself out, a pointed, elongating shape that seemed to be made entirely of shadow. Izzy squeezed her eyes shut and then opened them as wide as she could, willing them to see as clearly as possible. The pointed shape paused, and then began to unfold: it was an elbow, or perhaps a knee; she could see now that this was something's long, skinny limb.

Only then did Izzy remember her bargain with the Green Man. At that moment, sudden as oil tipped from a can, the Green Man poured himself out from the trees: his head and limbs unfolding from their huddled centre like a great spider unclenching itself, readying to run. When Izzy had seen him in the forest, the Green Man had been composed of the surrounding trees and bushes; to see him standing now almost clear of the woods altogether and taller than Izzy would have believed possible was an awesome sight. She couldn't see his eyes, but by the pointing of his chin he was looking over towards her, surveying the distance to the Hall and considering the challenge that faced him. She wondered if he could see her watching him.

Downstairs, the now-familiar sounds of the boggil had begun: here were the peelings and whisperings, and perhaps Izzy was imagining it but she heard a note of alarm in them tonight – something was different, the boggil could tell . . .

Suddenly the Green Man was on the move, swaying and hurdling across the driveway, riding the great chariot of his own limbs, a rolling cascade of branches and flung bushes, thrashing his arms for balance as though he were crossing a tightrope, and finally toppling over at full stretch until just his fingertips touched the ivy that grew on the walls of the Hall. Izzy had her face pressed to the windowpane; she was holding her breath so as not to mist it over.

Once he had made contact with the ivy, the prone form of the Green Man seemed to relax, and a ripple passed through him like a gentle wave reaching the shore. And then, as Izzy watched, he rolled himself up neatly like a carpet, until he was gathered into a bundle of sticks by the wall of the Hall. He had made it.

The noises from the boggil had grown increasingly frantic as the Green Man drew nearer: Izzy could hear it crashing and careering into one piece of furniture after another downstairs, its lurching movements accompanied by a nervous frittering sound and frenzied whispering. The Green Man was almost directly beneath her window now, so Izzy could just barely see him as his form re-emerged from its bundle, but she heard and imagined what happened next.

Eight spindly fingers and two spindly thumbs were easing the awning window in the parlour open a keek, and now the Green Man was beginning to slowly stretch himself through the gap and down to the floor inside. It was finicky work, posting in the branches and shrub clumps and pine cones that made up the Green Man's compendium, and seeing him uncoil like an impossibly huge fern's frond down from the window and into the room must have been terrifying for the boggil, who was racing from one end of the parlour to the other, yipping with fright like a small dog.

At last the Green Man was indoors. His many woods creaked and popped like arthritic knuckles as he gathered himself more tightly together, compacting himself into a tougher form in order to deal with the boggil who was now pinballing from shelf to mantle to floor to lintel to shelf, and squealing like a kettle coming to the boil. And then the chase was on: the Green Man leapt and the boggil sprang; the boggil leapt and the Green Man sprang. The sofa was punted out of position, the iron stew-pot clanged on the flagstones where it fell, the framed prints – Hedley, Jobling, Carmichael – rattled on the walls. Izzy listened to the racket from her perch at the window; as mysteriously as before, the noise did not disturb another soul.

Suddenly, with a clap, the parlour window burst open. Izzy pressed her face to her bedroom window, trying to get a glimpse of her tormentor when it appeared. Of course, she already had an idea what it looked like: to judge by the noises it had just been making, it must be something about the size of a football, and probably shaped more or less like a football, Izzy thought, with the merest stumps for arms and legs. It would be a dusty blue, the same colour as the kettle, and its body patchily covered in blue-black spines that would look like the chignon pins Mam used when she did her hair up . . . But somehow she had missed the boggil escaping from the window, as now there was a splash of pebbles skittering helter-skelter – it must have landed heavily on the driveway; but where was it? Izzy searched for a sign. It must have rolled straight into a sprint for the shelter of the trees. By now it was long since disappeared into the shadows, and Izzy would never see or hear of it again.

7

The Predator

I

It was the dog days of summer. In the walled garden, there were goosegogs and strawberries; and in the greenhouse, there were peaches – the most exotic thing Izzy had ever tasted. Time passed slowly and the heat was sticky, maddening, imprisoning. Dawn was the only time that had any freshness; by mid-morning the day's shape had been rolled flat as dough by the heat, and you were in danger of getting stranded in an ever-widening moment. Whatever she was doing, Izzy felt as she had when they lived in the Whindale valley, when she had stood alone up on the moors, exposed in the midday glare with little to see for miles in any direction and nothing that didn't swim in the haze, so that if she wanted any detail she'd have to focus on things close at hand: a blade of grass, or a ladybird, or the brown stippling of her grazed knee as it scabbed . . .

Izzy was, in fact, presently sitting on a tree stump by the chicken run, watching her hens picking and pecking at the kitchen scraps she had just thrown out for them. Nothing made her happier than simply strinkling a handful of grain or cabbage leaves for her girls, and watching them squabble over it. She had already washed and dried the dishes, put the crockery back in the dresser, cleaned the drain, scrubbed the sink, swabbed the cracked cement floor where it always puddled, and was now enjoying an interval of idleness while Mam took her afternoon nap early. In a bit, she'd rake out the coop while the hens were all out, and check for any eggs. It had been months now, and they'd only gotten a very occasional egg – just enough, in fact, to draw attention to the rarity of the event. Fortunately, it had been so hot that Mam couldn't be bothered to keep on about it. A holly blue lit on the ivy that coated the walls of the Hall and then, as though starting out of a dream, it capered off elsewhere. The air shimmered with the buzz of bees. Izzy thought, in summer you live the hours, and in winter you live the days.

2

The summer promised never to end, but time was passing. Heedless of who notices it, nature follows its course and the old pattern repeats. On Lammas Eve, according to the old calendar, Sheila showed Izzy how to make a cross of rowan branches tied up with red wool, to be hung on the lintel as a ward against the evil eye. They were sitting on the steps of the main entrance to the Hall, with Izzy trying to keep the Bairn occupied at the same time as making a cross. The problem was that the Bairn had decided that what he wanted – and nothing else would do – was the wooden cross Izzy was making. Izzy tried to distract him with his rattle and his teething ring, but that just seemed to make him want it all the more. Soon enough, he started to get twisty, whereupon Gerry appeared as though summoned, and said, 'Give him it. *Give him it.*'

Izzy handed over the rowan cross, and the Bairn settled to work contentedly pulling it apart.

From under the brim of her sun hat, Sheila watched Gerry stalk off with the Bairn in her arms, then looked at Izzy, eyes twinkling, and said, 'I reckon that lad's gonna grow up thinking his name's Givmit.'

Izzy covered her mouth with both hands: she had never heard anything so light-hearted.

'Anyways, we can easy make another cross. Plenty of wool . . .'

So Izzy set to work and made another cross. In truth, she had more faith in the Green Man than she did in Sheila's customs – it had been two peaceful months since the banishing of the boggil – but she played along because she liked Sheila. Sheila was a superstitious body: when she had to take Miss Claiborne her last cup of tea at night, she'd carry it to her with her pinny pulled up over her head, because she thought the portraits on the wall were staring at her. Dad had seen her do it.

Ray had spent the summer making the long-promised cot for the Bairn, but had devoted as much time as he could spare indulging in his new hobby (though Gerry would call it a 'craze' or a 'fad', depending on her mood), which was building and adapting cat's-whisker radios. They were ingenious things, needing no battery or any other power source to run. He had acquired a Bijou Crystal Receiver, dated 1924, a beautiful thing, and had cleaned it up and linked in an extra, bigger coil, which allowed him to pick up long-wave frequencies. The stations tended to overlap a bit, especially at night, which was the classic problem with the cat's-whisker method, but Ray was working on ways to separate the frequencies, and estimated that he'd be making another patent application in this area within three to four months.

For Annie, the summer meant being off school and having that much more time to spend with her horse, which she had named Bramble, and then renamed Gamble, and then briefly Campbell, only to revert to calling him Bramble. As long as the name rhymed, the horse wouldn't get confused, Annie reasoned. Gerry had suggested she call him Amble since that's all he seemed able to do.

Gerry's summer had just been one thing after another. Between running around after the girls and seeing to the Bairn, she was literally going spare. And those chickens were driving her up the wall. One bird in particular seemed to have it in for her. It sounded like a joke, but it wasn't funny. It always went for her, as soon as it saw her. Hobbs had witnessed such an attack on one occasion. He reckoned it was interested in her rings, and the buckles on her shoes, and the shiny clasp on her handbag, and so forth. Gerry had asked if he expected her to run around in the nude for the sake of the chickens, and what might this one peck at if she did? Hobbs had no answer for that. And then Gerry asked if Hobbs had noticed how foul-mouthed chickens are, and then she'd squawked, "Fuck-fuck-fuck . . . fuckoff!" Had a chicken delivered this joke to Hobbs, he couldn't have looked more surprised.

Anyway, eventually she'd got Hobbs to wring its neck and plote it, and she'd made a roast dinner that evening (Izzy and Annie peeling spuds and carrots while she balanced the Bairn on her hip and stirred the gravy), which made a welcome change from the dreary stuff Izzy usually served up, tripe-and-heel pie or Christ knows what. But what an absolute song and dance Izzy had made when she realised it was one of her precious chickens!

'Do you think that's the first chicken you've eaten?' Gerry had wanted to know. 'Do you? No. And what do you think the others died of, natural causes? I've never heard of anything so ridiculous. You're being utterly ridiculous. One chicken's the same as another!'

They weren't the same, Izzy had said; it wasn't the same when they were your own hens.

'Of course they're all the bloody same! There's nobody can tell t'other from which! Look, nitwit, a body keeps chickens so a body has eggs to eat. If the chickens won't lay, there's no point keeping them. And this is what happens.'

'What your mam means is, they're not pets. You can't go

round thinking of them as pets,' Ray had said, somewhat more gently – not that that did any good.

Izzy had said that she wouldn't eat it.

'You will eat it. You most certainly will. I haven't gone to all the bother of making this dinner for you to start being ridiculous and refusing to eat it.'

Izzy had repeated that she wouldn't eat it, not when it was her hen.

'I don't care if it's Henny Penny, you'll eat this dinner. You'll eat this dinner I've made. It's never bothered you before. What did you *think* you were eating when you were eating chicken?'

The exchange of views was kept up in this fashion until Gerry, eyeing her daughter meaningfully, served up. And if it had ended there, then perhaps the incident would not have come back to Gerry, unbidden, quite as often as it did, much later. But the remarkable thing was that, even once they were all seated at the table, Izzy could not be cajoled, shamed or mocked into eating anything – though all three techniques were employed. Izzy had never before been so stubborn. Annie looked at her sister wonderingly and shovelled some more food into her mouth. Ray's temper was slow to rise, but, as Gerry continued to fume and Izzy's immobile silence intensified, rise it did. Eventually, he thumped his fist on the table, which made the Bairn start to cry, and Izzy was sent to her room.

Gerry had even made a custard for after, and once they'd had that they brought Izzy back down and sent her over to Hobbs's cottage with a bowl of it as a thank-you.

Hobbs's cottage was one of a number of shielings to be found a short distance to the north of the Hall, most of which were occupied by people who had now retired from service there, and who, as Ray had explained to Izzy, paid Miss Claiborne a 'peppercorn rent', a phrase that Izzy had liked and had made sure to use at the next opportunity, which arose naturally enough when she was talking with Hobbs, as the two sat before a banked fire with a kettle on the hob.

'Well, the low rent's not just generosity. I don't suppose owt is . . .' Hobbs said ruminatively. 'Times is changing. Folk aren't as desperate for work nowadays. They're able to move around a bit more. If they don't like one job over here, well, they'll be off to get a different job over there. Miss Claiborne likes to keep the old retainers close. I reckon she hopes they'll hand on the old ways to the new breed, so to speak.' His opinion on the likelihood of this happening was clear from his tone.

Then he asked if Izzy had any news, but she didn't, so he asked her, while he ate his custard, to tell him again about how Annie got her horse, the details of which he found very amusing. But then the talk seemed intent on turning towards Izzy's hens, and a difficult silence descended.

'Well, you'll get a few broth out of it . . .' Hobbs found himself saying, but this didn't seem entirely respectful in the circumstances, so he changed tack. 'Mind, that was a canny custard. You can tell your mam I said that.'

'Mam says I make the plainest puddings she's ever tasted. She calls them my "here-I-am-where-are-you" puddings.'

Hobbs sat back and wiped his mouth on his sleeve. 'Now, is that necessarily a bad thing? A body might be just in the mood for a slice of "here-I-am-where-are-you pudding" . . .' Izzy smiled at that, so he expounded further: 'And, certainly, a "here-I-am-where-are-you" pudding is preferable to a *knavish* pudding any day of the week. A scholar once told me that much knavery may be vented in a pudding, and I've never had reason to doubt it.'

Hobbs asked if Izzy had any other news, and she said she'd seen a stoat the other day, and that set him on.

'A stoat skin was worth something when I was a bairn, but nowadays it'll hardly fetch more than a moleskin, and that's var-nigh nowt. At least, a *white* stoat's skin could be worth the bother of getting . . . Anyways, it's good that you saw one, as a stoat'll keep the rats down. Aye, a stoat'll take on a rat any day of the week. And if you've got chickens, well, sooner or later you'll be bothered by rats. Now, do you know how to tell a weasel from a stoat?'

Izzy shook her head – but now she was thinking of the Green Man, because Hobbs had just reminded her of the promise she'd made . . .

'A weasel is weasily told from a stoat, who looks stoatily different.'

Next morning, Izzy woke up thinking of the Green Man again. She had gone to bed thinking of him, and had woken up thinking of him, so she must have dreamt about him too; but she never remembered her dreams. She did remember, however, that he had asked her to do him a service, and that she had given her word. Today, she decided, would be the day she made good on that promise.

'Rid me of rats,' he had said – but the doing of it would be a complicated matter. Izzy came to think of it as a series of problems, none of them impossible, but each requiring considerable resolve to overcome. The first part, finding the gins, was quite easy: they were precisely where the Green Man had said they would be. But they were much heavier than Izzy had anticipated, and even dragging them, one at a time, as far as the cellar door was a taxing and noisy business. In order to get them from the cellar to the forest, Izzy landed on the idea of borrowing Hobbs's wheelbarrow. She was so sure that he wouldn't mind, she didn't think it was worth bothering him by asking. She didn't want to be a pest.

She'd have to wait until after Hobbs had knocked off for the day before she could borrow the wheelbarrow, so that's what she did. That evening she transported the gins into the forest, taking three in the first trip, and, when her shoulders and forearms nearly gave out in the effort, taking the remaining four in two further trips. She kept the gins covered with a blanket that the Green Man must have left for her in the cellar, and throughout the operation she tried to affect a matter-of-fact air, as though all she was doing was helping Hobbs – which is what she planned to say if she were asked. She found that, simply by telling herself – repeatedly and calmly – that this was all she was doing, she could almost make herself believe it, and it was the next best thing to being invisible: nobody gave her a second look, if indeed they'd given a first.

Each gin was attached to a stake by a chain, and Izzy drove the stakes into the ground at intervals along the riverbank of the Esh, hammering them in to their full depth with the heaviest rock she could lift. The next logistical challenge was to set them. Cranking open a hundred-year-old iron gin is no easy task for a little girl. She struggled with one of them until her fingers were raw, before noticing that each gin had a lever mechanism, but the rod was missing from the one that she had tried to open first. She soon found that five of the seven gins still had working lever mechanisms, and these were in fact fairly straightforward to open and set. She set the first of these before realising that she hadn't baited the trap, and wouldn't now be able to do so safely . . . Well, she had wanted to make sure that the ancient contraptions were still in working order, anyway. She found a long stick, and, lowering it between the jaws, used it to press down on the platform – nothing happened for several seconds, until she applied slightly more weight, and the mechanism was sprung: with an instantaneous eruption of violence the jaws clapped shut, snapping the stick in half and making the entire gin – and Izzy – jump. Her heart was pounding; she didn't know whether in excitement or fright.

Soon enough, the five working gins had been baited and set; the remaining two were less cooperative, but Izzy found that she was able to detach one of the rods from an already-set gin and use it to set the last two. At last, it was done: the riverbank lay in wait, primed and tensed, though only Izzy knew it. She looked up, for the first time in what felt like ages, and watched the Esh rushing along in endless frothy kisses, the shadows on the opposite bank deepening as the day drew to a close. The riverbank might have been baited with beauty. She let her breath steady. In a way, she felt that something had already been accomplished. It was a fine evening.

4

Next morning was a bright, sunny, complacent sort of day. Izzy took herself down to the river as soon as she could to check on things, to see what the night had brought her. She cut between the trees, swishing at nettles and rushes with the poker she was carrying. The closer she got to the Esh, the danker and more stultified the air became. A smell was beginning to rise – like wild garlic, though it was too late in the year for that, or some sort of decay that could still pass for sweetness. She thought, the river has bad breath in the morning. She herself had bad breath in the morning – Mam had said so. Annie had confirmed it.

As she approached the riverbank, Izzy could hear a sound like a kettle whistling; as she drew nearer, the noise resolved into various shrill screams, calling and answering and overlapping each other like the calls of some kind of terrible bird. Her hands were sweating, and she hadn't even got started. She gripped the poker more tightly, and crept closer to where the traps were laid. This is what she found: the first gin had been sprung and the bait was gone, but it had caught nothing; the second gin had a rat's leg in its teeth, but there was no sign of the rat; the third gin had caught a rat, and it was screaming; the fourth gin had caught a rat, and it was screaming; the fifth gin had been sprung and the bait was gone, but it had caught nothing; the sixth gin had caught a rat, and it was dead; the seventh gin had caught a rat, and it was screaming.

Five minutes later, and the riverside was peaceful. All was still, except for the shimmer of midges where they trembled above Izzy's sweating face like the atoms of the universe.

*

That night, Izzy, knowing that she'd get no sleep with the moon so full and the night so close, went for a walk in the woods. She moved between the trees in the warm nearly-dark, trying not to think about where she hoped to arrive or who she wanted to see, trusting that the old magic would work and she'd find herself happening upon either the Green Man or the Chapel. The trick, such as it was, consisted in keeping her mind utterly open and clear, but this was no small task in the forest, where there were always things to be noticed, even when the light was failing – like the spruce trees, for instance, looking furred with silver-blue needles of moonlight. Once you noticed something like that, you *thought* about it, and then, before you knew it, you were stuck there in the world that any fool could see. And that was okay most of the time, but right now Izzy wanted to escape from that world, so she decided to focus all of her thoughts on something that could now only be seen in her mind's eye: the long-since-vanished may blossom.

Izzy gave every part of her imagination to the effort of picturing exactly the may's particular hue of white, which wasn't perfectly white at all when you got a good look at it; it was green at the centre for one thing, or greenish, and not a very pretty shade of green either; and overall it had a greyish cast that spoiled the white, with the peppery, dusty look of the dark stamens before the petals. In the evening, the smell of it turned sickly; yes, may blossom was a subdued, melancholy thing when you thought about it, and even as she arrived at this conclusion a clearing in the trees seemed to open before her, and here – she glanced back, once, over her shoulder, as though she had a party of friends at her back – here of a sudden were the seven graves of the Claiborne children.

Now, you might expect a young girl, finding herself alone in such a place at night, to feel afraid, but Izzy felt nothing there but long-stilled peace. The gravestones were small and modest in proportion – so unlike everything else in Eshwood Hall, as though only the death of infants could inspire the Claibornes to restraint. None of the graves were tended, for who was there to tend them, apart from the forest, apart from the Green Man himself? All the same, none of the stones had toppled, or had even started to list, and moss had not yet covered over the names and dates that Izzy dutifully read – last-century dates for last-century names: John Percy Claiborne, Charlotte Anne Claiborne, Francis Merrick Claiborne, Cecil Bertrand Claiborne, Thomasina Sarah Claiborne, William Oswald Claiborne . . . Lost in this dolorous occupation, she didn't notice the Green Man when he first arrived. She turned from the final grave (which was that of baby Rupert, christened and buried with no middle name) to find him standing, head respectfully bowed, dappled in the moonlight that filtered through the branches of a sycamore.

Unsure of what to say, Izzy gestured towards the seven graves and observed that it was very sad that seven children should have died.

The Green Man shrugged. *Such . . . is nature's way. We must . . . allow it . . .*

'Did you know the children?'

The Green Man gave her a quizzical look. *Not while they were alive . . .*

Izzy decided to change the subject. She noticed that on this occasion the Green Man was sporting a jerkin of harebells, harvest daisies and harvest lilies – it was a princely adornment for the night of the Harvest Moon, and when she said as much, the Green Man seemed to swell with pride. She thanked him for scaring away the boggil, and he graciously accepted her recognition. Then she launched into the reason for her visit.

'I need your help with something else now. It's my hens. They're not laying, and Mam says that if they don't start soon she's going to sell them to the butcher. She's already killed one of them.'

Ah . . . blood has been spilled . . .

'Yes, so I need you to tell me how to make the hens lay.'

No easy task . . . but . . . I believe I can be of help . . . Still, a bargain must be struck, Isabella . . . Should I help you in this task . . . then you must help me with another . . . The hammer suffers as much as the nail . . . One hand washes the other . . .

This kind of talk made Izzy fidgety. She waited to hear the Green Man's terms.

Your hens must be protected . . . from a predator . . . that hunts in these woods . . .

The Green Man now had Izzy's rapt attention, so much so that she was almost disappointed when the fearsome predator was finally revealed, after one of the Green Man's characteristically extended pauses, to be nothing more than a fox. Still, the deal was agreed: Izzy would catch the fox. She could use one of the gins. The Green Man told her the best place to leave it this time.

But what about his side of the bargain? asked Izzy. He had yet to tell her how she could make her hens start laying.

In reply, the Green Man shuffled himself into a sort of shrug, and then said: *For this . . . you will need . . . item: Colman's mustard powder . . . one teaspoon . . . Also you will need . . . item: hot pepper flakes . . . Also you will need . . . item: one teaspoon of*

Marmite . . . Mix these things into their morning crowdy . . . Within two days . . . they will have gan to clock . . .

*

Up as ever before the rest of the family was awake, Izzy followed the Green Man's instructions to the letter, mixing the magic crowdy with a seriousness and ceremony that only a child can bring to such operations, until soon enough the hens were gobbling at their breakfast the same as always, unsuspecting of any difference . . . She watched them to make sure that they all got some of the special mixture, and was back in the kitchen frying bacon and tomatoes by the time her dad made it downstairs.

Izzy did not have to wait long to discover the results of her grand experiment. The very next day, she was delighted to discover that between them the chickens had, at long last, laid four eggs. As carefully as though they were gifts for a king, she carried the eggs up the stairs to the kitchen and presented them. The eggs were duly received, poached and eaten. Ray declared it the nicest egg he'd ever tasted, and that he was going to make a wooden box that Izzy and Annie could paint and decorate, and then they could put the spare eggs in there with an honesty box for pennies next to it. Or he could quite easily make a coin-operated mechanism that would dispense an egg, though that would take a bit longer. Either way, the hens would soon be paying for themselves.

As the Whippers enjoyed their breakfast and made their

plans, Hobbs could be heard outside, raking the gravel and singing a song to himself:

> *To hear the old men speaking*
> *Of a road too late for taking*
> *Would fix a mind on walking*
> *So why don't you and I,*
> *Oh, why don't you and I?*
>
> *The farmer and his widow*
> *A-walking in the meadow*
> *Share a single shadow*
> *So why don't you and I,*
> *Oh, why don't you and I?*
>
> *The daisies and the bluebells*
> *Tell their own sweet fables,*
> *They have no need of Bibles*
> *So why should you and I,*
> *Oh, why should you and I?*
>
> *May all our days be merry*
> *As Tom when he sees Mary,*
> *Tomorrow they will marry*
> *So why not you and I,*
> *Oh, why not you and I?*

8

The Bud

I

A fire blazed in the hearth. It was a good fire, but wasn't it
rather extravagant? Miss Claiborne would have to speak to
Sheila about it. But when was this – was this before Sheila?
Miss Claiborne thought it probably was. It was before
Sheila. But why, in that case, would Cookie have made such
an extravagant fire? And then she remembered: Father must
be away! Yes, that was it. Miss Claiborne was glad to get
things straightened out in her mind. And the fire was pretty
to look at, certainly. Of course she missed Father terribly
when he was away, but she also felt a thrill of truancy, the
sensation of being at large in the world. Not that she would
ever admit as much, but it was like a tiny rebellion. An uprising
of one. When he was home, Father had to have everything
his way. That came of being a colonel and it also came of
being a widower. Now Father was away because the war was

155

dragging on, Christmas after Christmas, and time had gone squiffy and nobody knew what year it was any more.

It felt as though it should be night-time, but the windows were flooded with light. Or perhaps she could see in the dark now? Oh, what was happening! Miss Claiborne reached for her bell-pull, but caught herself before tugging it. She was suddenly fearful. How very odd. She was fearful, she realised, because she didn't know who would be summoned. Would it be Sheila, or would it be Cookie, or would it be somebody else altogether? The light pouring in through the windows was stronger than daylight; now, how was that? Brash as sunlight on heavy fog. This was all very strange, to wake in one's bed and find a good fire laid in the hearth and all of this light trumpeting in through the windows and to be fearful of ringing the bell!

She could just hear, from several rooms away, voices and indistinct rumblings as of people moving around, going about their business . . . Quite a crowd by the sounds of them. There hadn't been a houseful at Eshwood Hall in ever such a long while, and now here were all these visitors and she was in bed missing all of the excitement. A man was laughing. That was an easy sound; she liked it. She did not like the sound of female laughter, on the whole, for if it wasn't whinnying it was shrieking, and a woman oughtn't to be heard making either of those noises. And then suddenly she recognised it as Dr Wintergreen's laugh, and then she remembered: of course there were people at the Hall, they were the soldiers, the dears from the line, and they were convalescing here at Eshwood! How had she forgotten this?

The Hall was a hospital now, taking care of the wounded. Not the wounded in body but the wounded in mind. And she was doing her bit, helping out here and there.

Strange to have found oneself, unmarried, thirty-four years of age, in a house full of men! Gentlemen. Military men. Strange to be suddenly looked for, called for. To be needed, after all. There was little enough for her to actually do, when it came to it. Fetch a glass of water, try to keep the maids organised, that sort of thing. Simply to be there was usually enough. But it was exhilarating, nonetheless. Dr Wintergreen had brought a gramophone with him, and when news reached them that the Armistice had finally been declared he played a wax cylinder of Vesta Tilley singing a song. Vesta Tilley! How excited the maids had become at the prospect of hearing their favourite music-hall performer on the gramophone. They couldn't have been more animated if the good lady had visited Eshwood Hall in person. It was a silly and, to speak squarely, rather a low sort of a song called 'Following in Father's Footsteps'. Miss Claiborne did not really approve, but the maids' rapture won her over. They all crowded around the machine to listen, and when it was over, of course, they wanted to hear it again, but this time they sang along, as earnestly as children singing a carol. It was a song with which they were all familiar, evidently. Well, after that they wanted to hear it a third time, and by then some of the more able-bodied fellows had come in, and next thing there was dancing. Miss Claiborne hadn't the heart to put a stop to it. She had even been asked to join in! She had had to decline the honour, of course. Unbecoming, to be seen dancing with a strange man, and to such a song, as though she were as giddy as the maids. Still, an officer had offered his hand. But no.

The fire roared and cackled. Miss Claiborne found that her hand now grasped the bell-pull. With an effort of will, she overcame the strange reluctance she still felt, and rang it. Such was the stillness of the room, it was hard to believe that a soul would come to her call. While she waited she mused on the just-audible murmur from elsewhere, the fire that needed no tending. Could it be borne, this interminable waiting? She rang again, more vigorously and more doubtfully than before, and still the winter sun, if that's what it was, poured in, and still the fog pressed up against the windows like the poor, like the Irish, like the shades of the maids and the footmen, like the revenants dressed up as soldiers and nurses, like her brothers and sisters and all the numbered ghosts of Eshwood Hall.

2

Saturday 15 September

Dear Mr Whipper,

We trust that this finds you in good health. Our legal representatives have on a number of occasions within the last year written to you demanding that you furnish the necessary information, plans and demonstrations required to perfect a variety of your extant patents as per the terms of your agreement. In the absence of said information, plans and demonstrations, we write to inform you that your patent applications numbering SG1245, OC7542, OC7591, WA55893 and LL324 are hereby rejected.

With regard to your latest patent application, dated September 3rd 1962, for a "resonant cord inductor electrical machine", we have, as per our standard practice, granted it an application number, LO1702. In the event that we receive an application for another similar machine or device, and this machine or device is proven to function in the manner described (and we must say, Mr Whipper, that we consider such an event unlikely to be realised), we will inform you, as per our legal obligation, so that you will have the opportunity to demonstrate the efficacy of your own invention.

As to your enquiry concerning the presence of government interests within the patent office, and the possibility of an applicant's ideas being either purloined or in any way interfered with, we strongly refute the insinuation. We would remind you that the Electricity Act of 1957 strictly prohibits the Central Electricity Generating Board from carrying out any function other than the production of electricity, and we consider the perusal of your patent applications to be an activity that falls comfortably outside that remit. We would like to assure you that no one but us will ever read of your inventions.

Yours faithfully —

Ray folded the letter back along its crease – it was heavy paper stock that they used – and replaced it in the envelope. He weighed it in his hand as he sat there at the parlour table, hearing the tick of the grandmother clock running slow but really hearing nothing, until the sound of Gerry's approaching footsteps began to draw him from his reverie.

Gerry burst in carrying the Bairn, who was wriggling to be free. The Bairn liked to play on the proggy mat, liked sticking his fingers in the holes between the knots of rags, and this he commenced to do as soon as his mother set him down. As she did so, she began telling Ray the news: Miss Claiborne was dead, she'd died in the night, and half the village was in the main Hall right now.

'You should get a shift on and see them – Sheila, Cowie, the lot of them – walking out with the family silver. Sackfuls of it. Brazen. You should see them. They must've had stuff stashed away, I reckon. They must've been waiting for the old girl to pop her clogs. That Sheila's a sly old bat. There's supposed to be an auction or a sale or something after the will's been read next month – that's if there's anything left.' Ray didn't seem to be listening. Since she was to have to spell it all out for him, Gerry added, 'You should get yourself over and grab something: everyone else is at it.' And then, feeling perhaps a little guilty, 'They reckon her heart gave way in the night. Yes, she just went to sleep and never woke up. For the best, probably.' And finally, 'It made me think of – of my condition. I hate to bring something like this, you know, back to myself, but that's what it made me think of, if I'm being honest.'

Gerry's voice sounded soft and fragile, but when Ray met her gaze, he found it to be as incisive as ever. There was, he became aware, something that he should be saying by way of reply, but he couldn't for the life of him think what it might be. Gerry had had enough, and, reasoning that if Ray couldn't be bothered to put in an appearance then she would have to, stormed out of the apartment as the grandmother clock struck a half-hour long since past.

Gerry saw Mr Wilkes by the library door. Wilkes was a shifty-faced bugger at the best of times, but today, carrying a bulging suitcase, he had special cause to look guilty. Gerry made sure to stop and say hello and get him to say what a sad day it was until the fool was sweating before she let him go. Coming out of the drawing room just as Gerry was going in was Sheila, clutching an oversized silver candelabrum to her oversized boobs. You couldn't accuse her of subtlety. Sheila was accompanied by her daughter, Biddy, who had recently acquired a crystal decanter and, long ago, her mother's incapacity to blush. Gerry wondered if Sheila would have an excuse lined up, but she'd underestimated her. Superstitious of sprites and fairies she may have been, but when it came to the traditions of service at Eshwood Hall, Sheila was their master, not their prey. There was a time for deference, and it had passed with Miss Claiborne.

'You want to get yourself in there and pick yourself something out,' Sheila advised, 'afore the old lady's friends and relations descend. There'll be a great raff of folk here the morn, you mark my words . . .' With that, Sheila swept magnificently by with Biddy in tow. Who was Gerry to argue? She headed for the breakfast room where there were some china figurines that she'd noticed a few weeks back; she might go and see if they were still there.

These particular figurines were a pair: a man and a woman in matching rose-pink and green outfits with gilt details. They could be arranged as though they were in conversation, as both had heads inclined as if to speak, and both held one hand to their mouth, as though there was something they wanted to say but couldn't. The textured folds of the man's rose waistcoat were especially fine. It would be a crying shame if they ended up being nabbed by the likes of Sheila. What use could she possibly have for them? Would she put them on her mantelpiece, next to her five-shilling clock? It would be worse than theft to leave them to such a fate, especially when Gerry already had a collection of pieces that you could compare to these. She'd recently lost a few of them to Izzy's ridiculous antics, and *that* wouldn't have happened if she hadn't been dragged all the way out here to the middle of nowhere, so Eshwood Hall owed her a couple of figurines: that was the way Gerry saw it. She opened the cabinet, took the figures, and slipped them inside her handbag; she'd already stuffed a scarf in there to act as padding. Then she headed outside for some air. It was like an anthill in the house.

Outside, Hobbs was sitting on a low wall by the orangery, watching the comings and goings at the Hall with what might have been amusement; it was hard to be sure of his expression as he had his pipe clamped between his lips. Gerry walked over breezily. The wind made her frock snap at her knees.

'Got your eye on anything?'

Hobbs's pipe remained preternaturally still.

'In the Hall, I mean. It's a free-for-all in there. Like Oldshield's High Street on Christmas Eve. Like Dublin on St Paddy's Day.'

Hobbs said that was fair enough for them that wanted

something, but as he didn't have need of trinkets, he'd be keeping out of the way.

Gerry found herself looking at him as though for the first time. His skin was still tanned from the summer, or probably it was always like that, from all the outdoors work. Brown as a nut. She couldn't help but compare the colour his skin had achieved to Ray's milk-white flesh. It was as though Ray had worked down the pit too long; something seemed to happen to miners, and even if they'd been out of that line of work for years, their skin always tended back towards that moony paleness it took on after months spent hidden from the daylight. She observed that it must be nice not to need anything, to which Hobbs replied that he hadn't said he didn't need anything, just that he didn't need trinkets. And somebody else's trinkets at that. After that he relit his pipe. Gerry sat down next to him and opened her handbag. Making a mock-guilty face, she produced the two figurines that she'd taken. Hobbs looked at them for a good while before he met with Gerry's gaze again.

'I thought I'd give them a good home,' said Gerry brightly. 'I have a sort of collection of them . . .'

'Bought or stolen?'

'Oh, you think I'm a terrible person! No, I bought all of the others in my collection. I don't have any men, though, so this would be the first one.'

'Hope your ladies don't fight over him.'

'Ah, they will, no doubt.' She turned them in the sunlight. The glaze looked pristine. Gerry then surprised herself by asking if Hobbs had always been a gardener, and learned that he had briefly tried his hand at service, being a boot-boy under the Colonel's valet, and then had done some pantry work and what-have-you, but soon saw that he wasn't cut out for it and he was happier outdoors, anyway. An easy silence formed, and when Hobbs spoke again it was quietly.

'I can't judge Sheila and Bob and that for helping themselves,' he announced at length. 'Fact is – well, the fact is they weren't born here, and the old lady made it known that that counted for something with her. So they'll know there won't be much pickings in the will for them. I can't judge them. There can't be many situations like this left anyway, so no use in letting a chance pass you by just so you keep your good name.'

'What about you?'

'There's nowt I'd want. Or do you mean the will? If I'm lucky, she'll've left us the wheelbarrow . . .'

'I meant, where will you go now, for work?'

'Oh, I'll probably stay on here. Aye, there'll be plenty of work, whoever takes over. And if they don't like the cut of my face, well, I'll take myself elsewhere. Always work for a gardener.'

Gerry returned the dolls to her bag, drawing Hobbs's attention back to them.

'Expensive, I suppose?'

'It varies. Dresden china. It depends on how old they are. Someone would know.'

'Someone usually does.'

While all of this was going on, Izzy walked into town. It would take her about forty minutes she reckoned, and half of that was driveway, which went by so fast in the car you wouldn't think it was especially long, but on foot it seemed able to uncoil twist after turn and turn after twist for ever, the loose stones kicking up before you and the cool tall trees parading on either side, and the gateposts never appearing up ahead . . .

Izzy always thought September was autumn, 'the embers of the year' as Dad called these months, but everything still looked like summer apart from the fact that the ferns seemed dusty, and some of the lower leaves on the trees – she stepped off the drive to inspect them – had had holes bitten into them by caterpillars earlier in the year that were now yellow and crisp at the edges like jigsawed puzzle-pieces.

She was going into town because Mam had sent her. Gerry had woken up that morning with her legs tingling something fierce, and the only help for it was Sloan's Liniment. Izzy had asked why Gerry didn't send Ray to fetch the liniment in the car, and Gerry had given her a warning look and told her that Ray didn't need to be bothered about every little thing, and besides, a thirteen-year-old was perfectly big enough to help her mam by walking into town and going to Gleghorn's. And she should make sure and get some new soap while she was at it – and not the usual coal-tar industrial-strength tallow Christ-knows-what, but something that was nicely wrapped, that smelled nice. 'If

I've got to live out here in the middle of nowhere,' she'd said, 'God knows I deserve a bit of something fancy now and again.'

Walking down the driveway, it struck Izzy that her own understanding of what smelled nice might be very different to Mam's. Izzy's favourite smell was strawberries, but she couldn't imagine a grown-up having that as their favourite. Maybe she would smell the soap in the shop and choose the wrong one. This idea gave her an uncomfortable feeling somewhere under her collarbones, and she swung her arms in big circles to chase it away. She saw some mushrooms coming up through the grass and she kicked their caps off as she passed.

She reached the gateposts with the big iron gates, and remembered when they first arrived, and how the poplars seemed to close in as the car turned in to the avenue . . . The gates were standing wide open now because there were so many people coming and going. Poor Miss Claiborne had died, and there would be no end of visitors, though she hadn't seemed to get any visitors when she was alive and that was sad. Izzy and Annie had been watching the cars come up to the house, and people coming on foot too, up from the village in the opposite direction from the way she was going now, as though she were swimming against the tide. Among the visitors had been Reverend Marshall, walking stiffly in his church clothes up the steps to the house. He must have seen tons of dead and dying people. With a shudder she imagined Reverend Marshall going in and seeing Miss Claiborne lying there, dead, still in her big bed, but motionless, maybe with her tongue sticking out and her eyes crossed. Or would she already be in a coffin? Izzy could only imagine Miss Claiborne lying in her four-poster bed, but they couldn't bury her in that.

The iron gates reminded her of the iron gins. The week before, she had taken one of them out into the woods again, and set it to catch the fox that the Green Man had warned her about. The next day she'd gone back to check, but it hadn't caught anything – though the bacon had vanished. She put fresh bait on it and set it again. When she went back next day the same thing had happened. So she tried once more, and that time, on the third morning, she'd caught him.

The gin had closed on one of the fox's back legs, breaking it. Even at a distance, Izzy could see the ends of the bone sticking out. It must have tried hard to escape, she thought, because the jaws had slid past the break and further up its leg. There had been treacly stuff all over its leg that Izzy hadn't realised was blood at first. Would it have tried to chew its leg off in order to escape? Some animals did that, but Izzy couldn't remember which ones. The jaws were probably clamped too far up its leg for it to bite it off anyway. It had been lying still at first, and she'd thought it was dead, but as she drew closer it had jerked awake and shuffled around a bit and started to make these yapping, mewling sounds that weren't like anything she'd ever heard from a fox before. More like a person trying to sound like a fox, she'd thought. Once she'd gotten used to the noises and they didn't bother her any more, she'd taken another few steps closer – at that, the noises had changed, and become more like dog barks or pig grunts. It had been trying to scare her then. That's what animals did, she supposed: first they tried to make you feel sorry for them, and then they tried to scare you. As she got closer still, the fox had started snapping at her, and the barking went up in pitch, until it sounded like a woman's shriek.

Now she was on the road. There were brambles in the overgrown hedgerows, but the remaining wild raspberries were dark and shrivelled, and the blackberries were still green. A month from now she'd be able to make Annie's favourite, blackberry crumble with burned edges. Here was a clump of corpse daisies, huge and stinking, a gone-over stench that was so fascinating she had to stop and take a few deep snuffing breaths to get the measure of how horrible it was – and then she ran for a bit to get away from it, but the smell seemed to follow her, as though it had caught in her hair.

The fox had snapped at her, but it hadn't been able to really do anything, even when she'd crept close. She'd brought the poker again to finish it off – quick work, stick work or poker work – but in the event she hadn't been able to kill it. Up close, she'd made the mistake of looking into its wild, amber eyes – and what she saw there wasn't fear or pleading, it was contempt: for itself, that it had let itself get caught; and for her, that she'd ruined it. In the moment that the trap had been sprung, even before the pain had crackled through its body, it must have known – Izzy felt sure – that it would never be well again, and that all its majestic fur, like all its fabled cunning, was for nowt. She supposed she'd felt sorry for it, which was silly, but there you go. Crouching over it, she'd suddenly, on a whim, dropped the poker, and stepped on the mechanism instead. The fox must have felt the pressure release – it had pulled its broken leg free and gone loping and lolloping off through the trees fast as it could. Well, she'd taught it a lesson, and that was good enough for now.

Izzy reached Eshwood. It was the first time she'd been here since May Day, and that was ages ago. There was the village green, looking smaller and less important, more diminished and bedraggled than she remembered from the fair – as if the fair had pushed the green outwards and made it bigger for a time, but in doing so had exhausted it. She crossed the grass quickly and headed for Gleghorn's.

Nodge was leaning against the wall outside the shop, eating a poke of bullets with all his might. Izzy hesitated. Would he remember her? She remembered *him*, of course, but it was months since they'd slid on the salt together, and she didn't reckon herself to be a very memorable person. But he looked up and shoved himself off the wall when he saw her.

'Haven't seen you in yonks. Where've you been?'

Trying to conceal her shyness and delight at having been recognised, Izzy shrugged. 'Just at home and that. What about you?'

'Dad's had us working like mad all summer.'

It was true, his hands and face were very brown. He shoved another sweet into his mouth. He was rewarding himself for his labour.

'You want one?'

She took a bullet, though she wasn't especially partial to them; they were just barely sweet, and faintly medicinal, she thought.

'How come you're not working the now?' she asked, around the bullet.

Nodge explained that today was Devil's Nutting Day, when you had to pick all the cobnuts you could find because they would have magical properties; but you had to make sure and only pick the ripe ones, because picking them before they were ripe was unlucky. Izzy asked where you picked them, and Nodge said there was loads down Backey Lane before you got to White Shield, and that was where he was going just as soon as the others turned up. He said that Izzy could come too if she wanted. There would be other lasses there, and that.

'I can't,' Izzy said miserably. 'I'm getting the messages for me mam.'

'Is she still poorly?'

'She'll always be poorly. She can't get better,' Izzy said, and immediately wondered, why not?

Nodge said he supposed that meant Izzy wouldn't be starting school next week, and when Izzy confirmed this he said that was lucky for her. He couldn't see what all the kings and queens of England had to do with him, and he was sick of having to remember their names and what order they came in and who killed who and when they died. This must have reminded him of Miss Claiborne's having died, and he asked Izzy if she'd seen her dead body. Izzy was sorry to have to disappoint him.

'Oh, well,' Nodge said. He told her about a sheep on his

dad's farm that had got knotted up in the fence wire and kicked itself to death before they found it. Sheep were forever dying, he said, and it was as though there was something that wanted them dead, because keeping them alive was no end of hassle. Hearing this, Izzy made a connection that felt like it had been a long time coming: there had been something, and there was still something, sheep-like about Miss Claiborne, with her dull, heavily lidded eyes and her chinless, puffy face and her hair hanging in ancient curls. And now she was dead, like the losing ram in the last bout on May Day.

Nodge asked what she'd to get from the shop, and she told him, and then he asked her how much money she'd got, and she showed him, and he surmised that she'd have enough left over to buy herself a tuppence mix-up or a bottle of Vimto and there'd still be a bit of change to give her mam. He led the way inside.

The shop was cave-like and smelled creaturely, with pyramids of tins rising like stalagmites, and a bell tinkled like running water when they went inside. There were so many little signs everywhere, propped or balanced or hanging from the ceiling, indicating everything from Woodbines to Wall's ice-cream, that it was difficult to see the things they indicated.

'You'll not be getting more sweets today, John Myerscough,' said a woman's low voice from behind the counter.

Nodge ignored this and showed Izzy where the soaps were stacked in their coloured cartons, the bright labels crowded together.

'Me mam likes that one,' Nodge said, pointing at some soap in a purple wrapper.

This was helpful, but not in the way that Nodge had intended. Izzy knew that Gerry would not want to smell like Nodge's mam.

'Actually, I think she's already tried that one,' Izzy lied. 'She's after something different . . .'

She picked up a white box instead, which was printed with 'Morny French Fern' in curly green lettering. The edges of the box were gold. She held it to her face and had a sniff, and though it did smell like any ordinary soap mainly, there was also a greenish smell about it that reminded her of walking in the woods where the ferns at the height of summer came up to your throat. It was the most expensive soap on the shelf. She took it to the counter, and asked the lady if she had some Sloane's Liniment too, and the lady got her a box and took the money Izzy gave her and didn't return any change.

'Too bad about the sweets,' Nodge said.

When they emerged back out into daylight, there were some other boys hanging around outside, three of them, all taller than Izzy, but a year or so younger, she guessed. When they saw Nodge, the tallest said, in a half-accusatory manner, '*There* you are!'

'Aye, here I'm is,' Nodge said. He didn't return his friend's gaze. Nor did he introduce Izzy to the others. Things were awkward for a moment until somebody said that Gavin had a new song for him, and so Gavin was cajoled into singing it. He was shy at first, or pretended to be, since Izzy was there and he didn't know her and she was a girl, but eventually he agreed to sing it, and this is how it went:

At the Cross! At the Cross! Where the Kaiser lost his hoss
And the eagle on his helmet flew away!
He was eatin' German puddin' when he hord the English comin'
And noo he's many a mile away!

Nodge made a snort, but it took Izzy a moment to realise that that was the entirety of the song – she'd rather expected a few more verses – so she didn't react, and then felt bad for not having reacted. But then it was okay because one of the other children said that that wasn't even the song he'd meant, and told Gavin to sing the other song, the rude song. And since everyone laughed at the word 'rude', Gavin did sing it, and it went like this:

Me bonny lies ower the ocean,
Me sister lies ower the sea,
Me daddy lies ower me mammy,
And that's hoo they got me!

Everybody found this very amusing, indeed some of the younger boys were doubled over with hilarity, all of which Izzy, though she was careful to laugh along with the others, found mystifying. And then Gavin announced that this reminded him of yet another song, which went like this:

When I was a laddie I lived wi' me mammy
And many's the howkin' me mammy give me,
But noo I'm a man, an' I dee as I can,
An' I dee to me mammy what she did to me!

Now everyone was hooting with laughter. Izzy copied them, squeezing her eyes shut and scrumpling up her nose. As they began to collect themselves again, Izzy felt Nodge move away from her until he was part of the group, which had already begun to drift along the street in the opposite direction from where Izzy was going.

'See you, Izzy,' Nodge called without looking back. They set off in earnest. One of the boys had a shopping bag that he was presumably hoping to fill with cobnuts, and Izzy realised that she had not asked Nodge what was magical about them. She wanted very much to go with them, but of course Mam knew exactly how long it took to walk to town and back, and if Izzy dawdled she'd get a hiding.

She watched the boys until, at the end of the street, they met up with three lasses carrying baskets. One of them, Izzy realised with a thrill, was the girl who had been the May Queen. Izzy gazed longingly at their pastel-coloured dresses, gathered at the waist with a belt – the latest fashion, she presumed. She considered her own everyday cotton dress that she wore day in, day out. When she looked up again, they had all turned the corner and vanished from sight.

The walk home did not seem to take as long as the walk into Eshwood had, and, despite knowing that her mam would be waiting, Izzy walked slower and slower the closer she got, until she was fairly dawdling along. She wished she could have gone nutting. She imagined giving her mam the things from the shop and then going out and taking Annie's horse and riding him all the way to Backey Lane, wherever that was. Then she would collect cobnuts for as long as she liked, and climb the trees with Nodge and his friends, and she'd be the fastest climber, faster than the boys even, because she'd had most practice. When it started to get dark, she'd jump back on Bramble with her pockets full of magical cobnuts and ride for miles and miles in some other direction, leaping walls and streams and fences and hedges all the way.

That was one thing she imagined. The other thing was going to school. Sometimes she imagined riding the horse right up to the school building and leaving him tied up outside, and other times she pictured herself simply walking there with Nodge and going inside when the bell rang and sitting near him in the classroom and learning the lists of kings and queens. She knew that Nodge found it all boring and she knew that when she had used to go to school she had said she found it boring too, but now that she was stuck at home with her mam all the time, she felt differently about it. Even Annie would be going to school next week. Maybe what Izzy wanted after all was to go to school as well. She wasn't sure, though. Or maybe she just wouldn't admit that this was what she wanted, so she wouldn't be so disappointed when it didn't happen. Because it was impossible: Mam needed her. But it seemed like Nodge's dad needed him too, to help on the farm, and he still let Nodge go to school when it was time. She wondered if she might be able to ask Dad about going to school, about whether she was really never going to go back to school ever again, or whether she might be able to start going if she did all the chores for Mam first thing in the morning or in the evening. She thought of this, knowing that when it came to it she wouldn't ask. Mam would never agree. Most of the chores weren't things that could be done in advance anyway. Izzy couldn't make ten cups of tea first thing in the morning and leave them lined up on the table for her mam to drink, or forget to drink, throughout the day.

Somewhere deep inside her, hidden as yet even from Izzy herself, there was a bud of something that might be going to blossom into anger.

4

A mustard-yellow truck was parked outside the Garland, and two men wearing green overalls were unloading barrels of beer from it. The younger of the pair, who (despite appearing nearly overmatched by the barrels) was doing the majority of the labour, was the apprentice, Mr Langley. The elder was the gaffer – and so called by everyone, so his name will not appear in the story. Down in the cellar of the Garland, peering up now and then through the open trapdoor, were the landlord and his brother-in-law, and old Mr Randall, who helped out on delivery day, in part to hear the news from neighbouring villages that was delivered at the same time as the beer. Loitering by the truck was Dixon. By his sour look, you might surmise that he was present because it was his job, and not because he wanted to be there; but that was the only expression his face had. In fact, apart from bits of day-work – topping beets and such in the season – Dixon didn't *have* a job, at least as far as the others could tell.

They were all discussing, or rather speculating about, the identity of the next incumbent of Eshwood Hall.

'Will hasn't been read yet, I suppose,' said the landlord.

'Hasn't been *proved*,' said Dixon.

'But they already know who'll be getting most of everything, and that's a chap called *Hesketh Pierce*,' said the gaffer. 'Heck of a name. Apparently, this Mr Pierce is set to come up from down south, and take a what-ye-may-call-it – inventory, aye – of all the bits and pieces at the Hall.'

'All the bits and pieces that's left, anyways,' said Dixon.

'There can't be a set of spoons in the place that doesn't have at least one piece missing as 'tis,' said the landlord's brother-in-law. 'Not a set of spoons, nor a set of crystal glasses, nor a set of owt what's not missing something. Owt Wilkes left lying, Sheila pocketed, I reckon.'

'I wonder how it came to be left to this Mr Pierce. Funny things happen when a rich body dies who doesn't have children . . .' said Mr Langley.

His gaffer answered him. 'Well, that's just it. There's some who've asked if Mr Hesketh Pierce isn't a bit more than Miss Claiborne's nephew . . .'

The men pondered this thought while Mr Langley hoisted the last barrel over the lip of the ramp and rolled it thunderously down into the cellar, where it landed in a nest of empty potato sacks.

'I don't remember seeing him about the place. I don't recall hearing about anyone called Hesketh Pierce. They made sure he kept a low profile if he was her son,' said Dixon.

'I remember him,' said a voice from the depths of the cellar. This was Mr Randall, who had remained uncharacteristically quiet until this point, in part because he had been waiting for this moment to come along, so that he could offer his contribution. 'I remember him coming up this way, oh, forty-odd year ago, when he was no more than a bairn. I was a stable boy at the Hall at that time – this was back in Colonel Claiborne's day – and I remember young Hess, as they called him, used to come up odd times for summers and Christmases, when the schools was holidaying, like. He used to act as a beater for the hunt.'

'Well, that settles it. Can't have been anyone's son if they had him as a beater. They'd've had him on a horse if he'd been somebody's son,' said Dixon, which effectively silenced Mr Randall.

'What sort of man is he, then, this Pierce?' asked the landlord.

'The sort with ideas. I'll tell you one of them. He says he wants the wood stubbed up,' said the gaffer.

'What? Hasn't he got enough plough-land to be getting on with as 'tis? Must be forty acres rough pasture even as 'tis,' said the landlord's brother.

'No, it's something else he's got in mind: *golf*. Aye, he reckons he's going to turn the place into a golf course. The Hall's to be a fancy hotel for the golfers to stay at.' The gaffer stopped work as he said this, and leaned on his staff. Seeing this, Mr Langley, who had started to load the cases of empties onto the back of the truck, did likewise, for there is no lesson an apprentice learns more swiftly than to follow his master when he downs tools.

'What the devil's his idea in that? I never heard anyone round here crying out for a golf course,' said the landlord.

'It's the future, he reckons. They say he already owns a number of these fancy sort of hotels with golf courses, so this'd be another one,' said the gaffer with a shrug. The others mused on this information in silence for a moment.

'Well, once it's his, he can do what he pleases, can't he,' said Dixon. 'Once the will has been proved.'

5

It was one week later, and Izzy was staring – unblinking, disbelieving – at the henhouse: at the wire mesh of the door curled like a sneering lip; at the feathers and the blood and the remains of the birds. She felt the ground shift as, in the light of the world's betrayal, old allegiances started to give. The rules were changing. The wind played lightly in the trees and far off a mistle thrush's song was briefly heard; then the silence flooded back. Izzy could feel herself sinking into it. Whatever emerged from that silence would emerge as a voice – as *her* voice – but what would it say? Beside her stood her mam, face fixed in a tight frown. That was the face Mam did when she wanted to disguise her real feelings.

Izzy had seen that look on Mam's face when Auntie Jean had phoned to tell her Nana Whipper had choked on her supper.

To her credit, Gerry felt no urge to laugh at what lay before her: it was a terrible sight, and no mistake, but what was the use in shielding Izzy from it? Such occurrences were in the way of things, as Izzy would have to learn sooner or later. Think of the cruellest thing you can imagine: the world has already thought of something crueller. And done worse. She wished that she'd learned that lesson earlier in life; it might have saved her a world of heartache. It had been a ridiculous idea to keep chickens, anyway. They could hardly keep themselves, let alone a gaggle of chickens. It was a bloody mess, though. It was all going to have to get cleaned up, and then that would be the last they'd hear about it, with any luck.

Beside Gerry stood Hobbs, who would have rather been anywhere else, but who, having chanced upon the scene on his way to dig up the last of the potatoes, had stopped, and had looked, and had seen – and hadn't been able to think of how to remove himself from the tableau in which he had been implicated as a witness.

'Aye, it'll a been a fox, most likely . . .' he said again, helplessly. The silence seemed to have closed around his chest like a great fist. Poor Izzy! 'Might've been a brock, though but. A brock'll do that to a henhouse, same as a fox will,' he said. 'Oh, yes. He likes quick pickings. He'll eat owt. Roots, grubs. Wasps! And he can be a finicky eater and all: a brock can pelt a hedgehog fast as you'd peel a banana!' Hobbs realised that he was talking too much, and to little purpose, but he felt he really had to say something, anything. Izzy had yet to drag her eyes away from the slaughter.

As heedless of Hobbs's words as she was of his abashed manners, Izzy felt the puzzle-pieces continue to slot into place, until she was returned to the desolating scene where the worst had already happened. All of her lovely hens were gone. A fox had killed them, and killed them just to kill, as foxes and – if Hobbs could be believed – other predators do. It had been the fox that she had failed to kill. She knew this. It had survived – maimed, furious, half-starved; it had crept limping here last night on its three legs, and it had set about gnawing and worrying the wire . . . She had given her word to catch the fox, and she had failed.

Gerry came to Hobbs's rescue. 'What he's saying, Izzy, is that – well, these things happen. It's just – it's nature's way.'

Izzy looked down: at her feet lay a scattering of black sunflower seeds and maize; a night sky of dark seeds spotted with light seeds that would never now be sorted from each other, which is what her hens had enjoyed doing more than anything. By an act of will, she raised her eyes and forced herself to look up, look away. She imagined an invisible hand holding her chin, keeping her gaze averted. The sky, at any rate, was almost clear. It was a superb blue, quite wrong for such a day. As she looked, the last trace of a lone bank of cloud broke up on the breeze.

9

Precious Little

I

Out of a fizzing mess of noise and a zipping and a zapping like the call of peewits, Izzy heard a brisk marching beat strike up, and then the warbling sound of a harmonica playing a simple four-note descending scale. Dad had a harmonica somewhere or other, a 'tin sandwich' he called it, but he'd taken it apart to clean it, and some of the reeds were now jumbled out of sequence. The warbling figure repeated a few times, and then suddenly there were voices, ghosts from the crystal: 'Love, love me too . . .' they seemed to be singing. She pressed the headphones more tightly on her ears. The song was ever so simple, but ever so interesting at the same time. The voices blended together just so, and made her mind go in more directions than one. Ray grinned, and he was pleased when Izzy grinned back – she'd been so glum lately, it was good to see her look a bit more cheerful.

Then the song disappeared in the snow of static and the faint beeping that Ray said was the submarines at Ulgh dockside talking to each other.

Ray started to explain how it worked: the galena crystal, and the cat's-whisker wire, and the ground-tuning dial, and the high-impedance headphones that you had to wear, and the aerial wire that he had installed a few weeks back when he'd been up on the roof to clean out the guttering. The best thing about it was that it worked for free: no batteries, no electricity. It was like he always said: there was energy in the air all around us, and we just needed the right instrument to capture it. Some day a fellow was going to invent a contraption that could do just that, and he'd be a very rich man, and the rest of us wouldn't have to work, or not so much, anyway. Although she always answered 'yes' when he asked if she was following him, Izzy preferred to let Dad's chatter wash over her. It was a reassuring noise. It was like invisible energy in the air.

They had passed much of the morning in the work-shed, Ray never happier than when tinkering with his inventions for an audience. Things were different at the Hall now that Miss Claiborne had died. Or rather, things were much the same, but they *felt* different now. At first, it had been all excitement: the week of Miss Claiborne's funeral had been the busiest that the Whippers had known since they arrived at Eshwood Hall. All day the kitchen had flashed and clanged with silver, pewter, brass, steel . . . But that had passed and now everything seemed to have an air of pretence, not that Izzy could have put it that way exactly;

but she understood that her dad and Sheila now seemed to be playing at their daily doings, rather than just going about them as before . . . It was clear enough that everyone was waiting for the new owner to arrive; then they'd see what was what, and whether they still had their old job, or a different job maybe, and whether the Hall was really going to become a hotel like people were saying. Izzy struggled to imagine the quiet (though never altogether silent) and half-decrepit old Hall that she now thought of as home becoming a bright, new hotel forever full of strangers. Those corridors – which, though forbidden to, she had walked at night, many times, candle in hand, inhaling the cold night-breath of the place, watching the great wheeling shadows flicker up and down the walls around her – how could they ever be lit with anything so steady and stultifying as an electric light? And as for the idea of anybody chopping down Eshwood Forest, it was painful to think about. It was *impossible* to think about. How could anyone look at a forest and imagine it not being there? The trees' fate hovered, close but mysterious, already decided somewhere by somebody, so that the now felt like the meantime.

It had been an unseasonably mild, dry October . . . What a strange year! It had taken so long to get spring started, and now summer was running late. What would that mean for the coming winter? Sheila would surely have an opinion on the matter. Izzy was walking now from Dad's work-shed back to the Hall, with the low, midday sun winking in each of the windows in turn . . .

Unbeknownst to Izzy, or to anyone else at the Hall or the

Garland for that matter, Miss Claiborne's will was proved at Oldshield that very day, with her estate valued at £172,268.

2

Hesketh Pierce was starting to lose his patience. First, there had been the pictures: where was the Correggio of *Peter Denying Christ*, with the carved gilt egg-and-tongue frame? Where was Barocci's *Agony in the Garden*, with the carved gilt gadroon frame? And where in the name of everything holy was Jekyll's *Dwarf Servant Holding Pineapple*? Next, the books: Hesketh didn't care a fig about them, quite frankly – they were hardly worth the bother of auctioning, that was his opinion on the matter, anyway, but nevertheless: there was barely a score of titles that seemed saleable. He was standing in the library now, shaking his head at the volumes before him on the table and occasionally shooting a glance at the most insolent footman he'd ever encountered, 'Wilkes' or some such name, who was regarding him as steadily as a pickpocket. O'Donovan's *Annals of Ireland*, Wilkins's *Life of Castlereagh*, Fergusson's *Tree and Serpent Worship in India*, a portfolio of *Vanity Fair* cartoons, a roller map on linen of Canadian railroads, a map (unmounted) of the Northalbion mail roads . . . Could these really be the choicest cuts from the Eshwood library? Hesketh abruptly turned his back on Wilkes, and marched up to get a look at the books still on the shelves. Peering over his spectacles, he let his eyes drift over the less familiar titles: *Verus Jesuitarum Libellus*, *Clavicula Salomonis de Secretis*, *Sepher Maphteah Shelomoh* . . . It hardly seemed likely that buyers would be found for dusty old volumes of Latin and Hebrew. Perhaps they could be donated to the local boys' school?

It was a book that had started the business, truth be told. Hesketh may have held on to a handful of fleeting memories of visiting Eshwood Hall as a young boy, but he was reliant, to an extent that he didn't care to make generally known, on a volume in his possession, *The Treasures of Eshwood*, written by Colonel Claiborne in his dotage. And the more time Hesketh spent picking through the actual detritus of the Hall, the more he was coming to doubt that the fellow had been in his right mind when he wrote it. Hesketh pictured him, wrapped in a rug by the fire, stewed, furiously elaborating his family history, decorating the Hall with every trinket he'd ever coveted . . . The old fool must have been consoling himself with this production at just the time of Hesketh's boyhood visits, and the really irritating thing was that, although Hesketh couldn't recall the Colonel himself, he had in the intervening years become so familiar with his written account, that he now possessed deeply untrustworthy memories of having actually seen some of the treasures with his own eyes. Almost fearfully now, he wondered: had his fingers ever in reality touched that embossed Delftware pap jug? The business of the day, it was becoming clear, lay in distinguishing between varieties of absence – in particular, between the missing and the never-was – and doing so before they all bottomed out into the irretrievable-in-any-case.

He had been fairly dragged into all of this. Now here he was, having driven all this way, given no assistance apart from a worse-than-useless footman, and Mr Stopford, the auctioneer, was due in an hour and would be expecting the catalogue to be complete . . . Hesketh turned back to his work in dismay.

Although there was no sign of the obviously fantastical sundial, upon which *The Treasures of Eshwood* lavished pages of tedious rhapsody, in general the items to be auctioned under the headings 'Furniture, Carpets, Laundry and Outdoor Effects' seemed to be in order. That could, of course, have more to do with the impracticality of making off with a chaise longue than anything else. But it was when he came to the categories 'Silver, Plated Ware and Glass', which had been amassed for his inspection in the breakfast room, that Hesketh began to grow really suspicious. What had become of the six Indian filigree eggcups, the gilt coronet band? Why was the William IV shell-pattern table service missing its silver sugar sifter, ladle and tongs? Why were all four of the Georgian thread-and-fiddle table services missing their gravy spoons? He hadn't been surprised to find the six gilt chamber candlesticks (plus snuffers and nozzles!) missing, but he could have wept at the absence of the Bohemian opal glass floating rose bowl, not to mention the tiny old silver-gilt bijouterie box that he *knew* Auntie had kept on her bedside table.

'Now. "Ornamental Items, China and Miscellanea". We shall have to let the clocks run down. One cannot auction a ticking clock. Do you understand what I'm saying?'

Wilkes looked sheepish. 'Yes, I understand you, Mr Pierce. It's just that, well, I think the clocks, or most of them, have already been let run down. Miss Claiborne kept to her bed that much in her final years, it hardly seemed worth the bother to keep winding them . . .'

What had the staff been *doing*? Whatever precious little it was, they had evidently done less of it since the old girl died. Had she *ever* been able to get work out of them? It was impossible to say. Time, it was evident, had fallen asleep in Eshwood Hall. Well, now he, Hesketh Pierce, was going to wake it. He considered saying as much, but frankly it would be wasted on this dull-eyed wretch of a footman. He would say it later, to someone else. Right now, he felt that it was time to bark something authoritative at Wilkes, so he said, 'Fetch me the ladder, would you? I want to see the upper shelves . . .'

Wilkes cleared his throat. He did not move. 'I would do so, sir, with pleasure, but the only stepladder I know of is currently on the roof.'

'A library without a ladder! On the roof? What the devil is it doing there?'

'Mr Whipper left it there, sir.'

'Who is Mr Whipper when he's at home?'

'The chauffeur, sir.'

'Look here: why did the chauffeur put the stepladder on the roof?'

'He's also the odd-job man. And he was up on the roof to erect an aerial, sir, which he's going to use to draw energy from the atmosphere. That's according to him, sir.'

'He said this to you? The chauffeur said this to you?'

'That was the gist of what he said, insofar as I understood it, sir.'

Had everyone gone mad? Was Eshwood Hall, in fact, a madhouse? It might be. It had the look of some sort of institution. Perhaps (the idea blazed across his mind like a comet from God knows where) he could turn the place into an asylum. There would be more money in golf in the long term, certainly, but it would cost ever so much more to establish a links in the short term. He had a vision of lunatics wandering happily in the woods. He dismissed the idea utterly.

After this there were still 'Curtains, Linen, Mattresses and Cushions' to consider: whether these categories had fired the imaginative senility of the Colonel, Hesketh would soon surmise. Probably a hundred items, all told.

Wilkes had remembered something: would Mr Pierce be wishing to examine the basement effects?

Hesketh poked his spectacles back into place. No, he couldn't believe that there would be anything especially valuable to be found in the cellar. He simply couldn't believe it. There was no wine down there, certainly: he'd checked already. He'd skip that category altogether and save himself some time. Hesketh was really starting to lose his patience.

3

An hour later, Izzy was running through the woods, the blood pounding in her ears and humming in her teeth. The Green

Man would be waiting for her in the Chapel. The Green Man would be waiting for her in the Chapel: she knew this, though she didn't know how she knew this. She would come to the Chapel if she only kept running, and it didn't matter in which direction she ran.

She had heard the man talking to the other man about chopping down the forest, and suddenly, as will happen in a child's understanding at such times, a number of inchoate fears had congealed. Now urgency had her in its grip. The prospect of the trees being felled had seemed a distant one, but Izzy saw that it could be about to start this very day. It was of paramount importance to tell the Green Man what was happening – why hadn't she told him sooner? He would surely know what to do. He must have defended the forest from such attacks before.

Branches whipped by, bracken sprayed where her feet slipped, but fear was catching up with her, however fast she ran: fear that, by failing to kill the fox, she had been banished once and for ever from the Chapel and from the Green Man's company. Had it ever taken this long for the Chapel to be found? Of one thing she was certain: if she were to start *looking* for the Chapel, it would remain hidden. It had to want her to find it. She ran on in that hope. But it is hard to hope for something you mustn't think about, and it is hard not to think of what frightens you, for fear of it coming true. And then, sudden as ever, and exactly where she wasn't expecting to find it, there it was.

With a shock, Izzy saw that the front door was open a

crack. She had never yet managed to get that door open, so there must be someone else there – perhaps they were still inside? She crept closer, trying to feel reassured by the eerie calm that the Chapel seemed to exude: surely this meant that it was standing empty . . . She reached the door and peeked into the gloomy interior.

There, regal, magnificently idle, the Green Man lounged upon the great wooden chair, his head propped on one hand, his body resplendent in fallen leaves that showed in every colour from holly green to the blood red of the maple. Still as a sculpture he sat, and a sculpture is what he might have been just at that moment. He was alone, as he had always been alone when Izzy had met him, and yet as she crept inside the Chapel she found herself all but holding her breath. She leaned her weight on the door to push it to, and the sinuous vines of the Green Man's limbs began to stir and tighten as she drew closer . . .

Izzy still wasn't sure that the Green Man was fully awake when, having prepared herself to tell him about the horrible men who were coming to chop down the trees, she heard herself say, 'I want you to fix Mam's heart.'

The eyes opened. Today they consisted of two small, white, waxy mistletoe berries, and the way they glowed in the shadows of his eye sockets gave him an unearthly look. *Your mother is . . . heartbroken?*

'Yes. Sort of. She has something wrong with her heart, which is why she's always in a bad mood, especially in the mornings, and she can't do any work.' Izzy searched through her thoughts, and found that she had surprisingly little further information on Mam's condition. 'Sometimes she says things she doesn't mean,' she added.

The Green Man frowned and shook his head, until a wasp lazily freed itself from the twigs there, and buzzed briefly down to the floor where it crawled about drunkenly. *Now, why . . . should your mother's heart . . . be of such importance to you?*

It was a fair question, and Izzy answered it as fairly as she could. 'I want to start going to school again, and I can't go unless Mam gets better, because she needs me to look after the Bairn, and that.'

The Green Man thought this over for a moment or two. He watched Izzy while he was doing this. *It sounds to me . . . as though you want me . . . to save your mother's life?*

'Yes! I mean, yes, if she's in danger—'

Ah! She is . . . of course she is . . . If her poor heart doesn't kill her . . . I don't know what will. The Green Man frowned again; the bark of his brow crumpled together. *But of course you know . . . by now, certainly, you know . . . that a bargain must be struck.* At this, as his small, white, eager eyes met Izzy's, and one idea encountered another, she felt the temperature drop. *Only a life . . . can pay for a life . . . Isabella Whipper.*

For the first time since she had met the Green Man, Izzy felt afraid. What was he getting at? But she had a feeling that she in fact already knew what he wanted, and was only pretending to herself that she didn't understand. There wasn't a sound from the forest outside: the birds had ceased their song and cocked an ear to whatever happened next. Izzy looked around the Chapel as if hoping for help, but the statues were only statues and didn't budge. The Green Man wiggled his little finger into what was presumably his ear, and drew out a glob of sap. Forgetful of Izzy's being there, he gave it a cursory sniff before wiping it on the arm of the chair in which he sat. Izzy brought him back to himself by asking what exactly he'd meant when he'd said that only a life could pay for a life. Whatever he was after, he was going to have to come out and ask for it.

Why, I want the child, he said easily. *'The . . . Bairn' . . . as you call him. Little Raymond . . . Raymond Junior . . . I want him.*

4

'I've told you, it's a surprise!' Hobbs was leading Gerry through the woods.

'Tell me we're nearly there at least. We must be nearly there by now. My dress is going to be fucking ruined!'

'Mind, you've got a dirty mouth on you, haven't you?' said Hobbs with some amusement.

'Didn't realise you were so prim and proper. Don't you get bad language this far north? Go on, say it: eff you see kay. *Fuck.*'

'I never heard a lassie talk like you. Never heard the like.'

Gerry, sniggering a little nastily, asked if it upset him, at which Hobbs grinned.

'Not really. I reckon I could get to like it. Anyways, we're var-nigh there . . .'

Gerry stopped to look at him, this man she was out walking with, alone in the woods. Christ, he could hardly speak English. What the fuck was she doing? Hobbs, turning to see why she had stopped, saw the look of disgust on her face, and guessed all that lay behind it. Grinning again, he at once affected the poshest accent he could muster – and it was a surprisingly accurate one, to Gerry's ear, probably because his late employer had given him ample opportunities to hear one and learn it and mock it.

'I mean to say, we're very nearly there, Miss Geraldine; I mean to say, we approach—'

More sternly than was strictly necessary, Gerry instructed him not to call her that.

'*Geraldine*: that's your name, isn't it?'

'*Gerry* will do.'

'Aye, Gerry'll do, but on your birth certificate it'll say—'

'I don't give a tinker's cuss what it says. I hate that fucking name. Christ, *Gerry* is bad enough.'

In truth, such words on a woman's lips shocked Hobbs, but he hid this by looking bemused at how quickly Gerry's mood could change, and muttering, 'Hell's bells and buckets of blood!' to show that he, too, could curse.

At last, they arrived at their destination, the Chapel. Hobbs had brought them from the most favourable approach, and the Chapel was looking especially attractive in the late-afternoon sunlight. He gave Gerry a moment to appreciate it.

She had just realised something: 'This is what you spent the war doing, isn't it? Planting trees for the Forestry Commission, yes – planting trees and finding good places to fuck the wives of the men who were off fighting? That's it, isn't it?'

She was laughing now; laughing at him.

'Had a good war, did you? While the real men were off fighting, you were off fucking. That's all you're good f—'

Hobbs, finally angered by her games, grabbed Gerry by the shoulders. 'Aye, and I can imagine you, growing up with six older brothers – all of them babying you and wrapping you in cotton wool, turning you into just the sort of spoiled bitch who drops her knickers the second her husband's back's turned.'

Gerry stared at him for a beat, then gave a shriek of laughter and planted a kiss on his mouth that left hers zinging with the taste of blood.

*

Inside the Chapel, the sound of people approaching awoke Izzy from her reverie and into a sudden panic. She wasn't meant to be in the woods alone. She was going to catch hell. She'd get another hiding. She searched for a place to hide, and as she looked, she became sensible of the fact that the Green Man had vanished – just dissolved, quite suddenly and silently, into the leaf mould and the branches lying strewn on the floor. Izzy could see nowhere for her to hide except behind the main door. She would just have to hope that if anyone came in, they didn't close the door behind them. She waited there, braced against the wall.

*

'So. Here we are. Bonny, eh?'

Gerry, caught off guard, might have seemed momentarily

impressed by the Chapel's strange, tumbledown beauty, or perhaps she was – just for a second – troubled by the sight of it, and the way it seemed somehow more *real* than its surroundings, as though it had been superimposed, or was in better focus than the trees around it. In any case, she composed herself almost immediately, and observed that it would do, that it would serve its purpose. And when Hobbs asked what purpose was that, she explained that, sadly, she couldn't say without using the sort of language that he didn't like to hear.

'I never said I didn't *like* it . . .' said Hobbs, moving close to Gerry, speaking more intimately. 'Say it again . . .'

Gerry looked at him, or, you might say, gave him a look; it was a sort of sneer, and it had the effect it always had: Hobbs felt something rise within him, or, you might say, he felt the forest floor tilt, and now his mouth was pressed to her mouth and he felt her hot, quick tongue.

'Say what?' Gerry whispered, 'Fuck? Fuck! *Fuck me . . .*'

'Fuck . . .'

'Fuck my cunt, fuck my cunt,' whispered Gerry, her breath wet in Hobbs's ear.

With a crash, the door to the Chapel burst open, and Hobbs staggered inside with Gerry giggling after him.

*

Izzy pressed herself even more tightly against the wall behind the door, which, flung open, now stood only inches from her face. Through a crack in the wood, she saw a kicked pebble skitter across the floor of the Chapel, and two figures come inside. They were leaning on one another for support, as though wounded or in drink. Izzy's heart was thundering in her chest, and she could feel the blood pulsing in her neck and ears, and only now did she recognise her mother and Hobbs, though it was more than she could do to speak, even had she wished to. They were pulling at each other's clothes, and Hobbs was holding Gerry's hair in his fist. Slowly they collapsed into one another and sank to the floor.

And then, as Izzy watched, Hobbs, crouching horribly over her mother, began to writhe and shiver, as though he were shaking free of something, and then – then it happened. The branches and leaves began to sprout, first from his mouth, and then – as his back arched, and his chin pointed up – from his nostrils and ears, even from his eyes, spreading out in vines and tendrils that covered his body and curled caressingly around Gerry. Izzy bit her knuckles as tubers twitched and nosed out here and there, emerging now from every pore of Hobbs's body, slithering out until they struck a pillar or a pew, whereupon they began to worm and wind around them and engulf them too. The Chapel was transforming into a bower; the forest had come indoors. Izzy watched from behind the door, aghast. The Green Man was attacking her mother – he was killing her, consuming her, for Gerry's writhing body was disappearing under the thickening foliage; her face, caught in glimpses, was contorted in what, to Izzy's eyes, looked like pain; and surely the sounds she made were cries of suffering.

And then, just at the moment when Izzy could stand it no longer, a sudden chance opened like an eye. Easing herself out from behind the door, she slipped from the Chapel unnoticed. Within seconds she was running home through the woods – and didn't the branches seem to reach for her, the brambles embarrass her, every stray stone try to trip her? For the woods, she knew, had meant for her to stay; they had wanted her to see them eating her mother. They were furious with Izzy, furious that she had refused their bargain. It was all, all of it her fault: she had asked the Green Man to mend Mam's heart, and he had kindly and graciously offered to do so – but she had been impittent, and had refused him, and now he was claiming her mother for himself and eating her alive.

Izzy reached the Hall and charged up the stairs and up the stairs and up the stairs and burst into her parents' bedroom. There was the Bairn asleep in his cot. There was the Bairn, not a soul to look after him. Izzy kept still and waited till she had caught her breath, waited for her racing heart to steady. She had always preferred the Bairn when he was asleep. He looked like a doll, then, and he didn't mind being picked up (she was picking him up now). In fact, everyone seemed happier when the Bairn was asleep. He was like a puzzle that you had to solve, and you knew that you were on the right track when he went quiet, and then, once you'd got him asleep, you'd won. Izzy had never thought of it like that before, but she did now, as she carried him down the stairs one at a time and out of the house, shading his eyes from the sun because of course you had to keep him asleep once you'd got him asleep, else it was all for nowt.

Soon enough she was carrying him through the woods, past the buckler ferns that were still green and fresh in the shelter of the riverbank hazels, past the tall willow wands with the leaves that fluttered like ragged pennons as she passed. And didn't the branches seem to part for her, roots snuggle down in the thick dark moss so as not to trip her, the birds hush up as though the trees had whispered *whisht*? No sound now but the giggling waters of the Esh. The woods, she knew, wanted this. She was doing the Green Man's bidding, she was making amends, it was all, all of it going to be well.

Down in the dell, Izzy knelt with the offering she had carried so carefully. All that was done was lovingly done, she thought – or no, she hadn't thought that yet, because this was happening, yes, but it was also a memory she was laying down, now, planting down, bedding down for later; like Hobbs with his beets and neeps and his second earlies, she was planting a memory – here amid pocketfuls of fallen chestnuts – that wouldn't show for a while yet. A red dead-nettle, a white strawberry, a little yellow tormentil . . . Summer flowers, still blooming here in the dell! The dell was the heart of the forest. The Bairn was the shard of ice in the heart. Fleabane. Knapweed. And all that was done was lovingly done – where had she heard that? Had she heard that? It sounded like something the Green Man would say, so that must be it. Yes, that was it, and now here was a sort of bed of lush grass and simples – wild chamomile, blue veronica – so she lay her brother down. Lovingly down. And here was eyebright, and here was herb robert. Would he wake when she unbuttoned him? Surely not, when the dock cress was so soft, and the dell, even now in October, as warm as blood.

'I don't know, a bloke like that. I don't know. All he's about is giving himself an easier life.'

'He's very good with the girls. They'd have me running around like a maniac if he didn't keep them in line. He's very good that way. A lot of men don't get involved, they just leave it to mother, but he's very good.'

Gerry and Hobbs were lying on two pews that Hobbs had shoved together so they formed a sort of cot. He'd draped them with a blanket that he'd brought along with him: its coarse wool was prickling Gerry's naked flesh, a curious but not entirely unpleasant sensation.

'I suppose there's lots of ways to be a man in this day and age, but I don't know,' Hobbs said again. He was lying on his back, gazing up at the array of foliate heads and angels that decorated the roof of the Chapel. The sweat had cooled and dried on his skin and the air was beginning to feel chill, but he wasn't about to complain, with Gerry's warmth by his side.

Gerry had no religious convictions to speak of — raised as a Catholic, she'd left all of that nonsense behind her as soon as she was able; she attended church at odd Christmas-times and Easters out of curiosity more than anything – but she nevertheless found that the smell of sex in the Chapel had a sacrilegious thrill to it. She preferred it to what the priests used to get out of their thuribles. That sounded so funny, she nearly said it out loud, but thought better of it. This lump wouldn't know how to take it. That was another thing about Ray: you could have a laugh with him.

'I think he's like one of his inventions; he pays for himself . . .' she said vaguely.

'Well, I can't blame you, that's all I'm saying. Nobody can blame you.'

Gerry shifted her weight, and felt the blanket scratching more insistently at her. She'd have to be careful not to end up with a rash. 'Christ, what is this stuff, wire wool? Did you get it off the back of a tractor?'

Hobbs lifted her with one arm until she was lying all but on top of him, with as little of her delicate flesh as possible touching the blanket. He held her steady with one hand on her backside. 'Better?'

Gerry nodded and smiled, and rested her chin on Hobbs's chest. She let the silence build and spread. Breathing in time with him, this was what she liked: just lying quietly together. Although it was women who had the reputation for nagging, in Gerry's experience it was the men who always spoiled things with a lot of talk. A minute or so passed peacefully.

'It's like those figures up there,' said Hobbs, fixing his gaze on the roof once again. 'Some of them's angels, and some of them's – well, not devils exactly, but certainly not angels either. And they're fighting the fight between themselves, and who's going to win? Nobody knows.'

Gerry closed her eyes. Hobbs was, she supposed, trying to think. They were going to have to talk. She opened her eyes.

He went on. 'And who's going to judge the final outcome? Well, not me. And if a woman like you has had enough of a man like that, well, I can't say I'm surprised, that's all I'm saying.'

'Whoa, there . . .' said Gerry quietly, propping herself up on one arm and realising as she did so how chilly the Chapel had become. 'Listen, it's too cold to be lying around in here like this. I don't know about you, but I'm frozen. I'll have to get dressed . . .'. As she collected her things, Gerry tried to maintain the matter-of-fact tone when she moved on to discuss more personal matters. She had not, she explained, had enough of Ray. She wasn't planning to leave him, that was for sure. She was in no position to do so, even if she were so inclined.

'Well, I could help you to get *into* such a position,' said Hobbs, guessing that this is what she wanted him to say. '*I* don't work for nowt. *I* don't "pay for myself". And I've got a few bob saved up, like.'

'Listen. Now, listen. You're very sweet. You are. And I know you mean what you're saying. And what we just did, it was lovely. It was just what I needed. What I wanted. But what I *don't* want is you thinking that this means I'm going to up and leave my husband and kids, because I'm not going to do that. It wouldn't be fair on you, and it wouldn't be fair on them.' She looked him right in the eye as she said this. That was something he'd remember later.

'So that's it and all about it, eh?' Hobbs managed to say.

'Don't be like that. Be nice. I thought this was going to be nice.'

The moment stretched until it felt horribly taut, and then the tension broke as Hobbs heaved himself to his feet and muttered that he didn't know what she was like, didn't know what she was after, and things like that. He pulled his shirt across his shoulders. He scratched his head and gave a loud sigh and said, 'Never heard the like . . .' with something like the bemused exasperation he'd shown in response to Gerry's cursing on the way to the Chapel. Gerry felt an enormous relief that it was going to be all right. Hobbs shook his head, looked for his trousers, and scratched his balls.

6

Water gurgled in the pipes, finding its level. Izzy listened to the tick of the bubbles as they jittered after one another, and thought of how tirelessly water moved; how it moved until it had placated itself. She was sitting at the table in the parlour, gazing out of the window over the expanse of the treetops and the cloudy, livid sky above. When she turned back to the quiet room, it felt eerie. It was as if Mam's chair, and the clothes horse, and Dad's Pye Black Box had suddenly acquired an air of make-do and impermanence – they had been arranged, like props on a stage. A family had been encamped in these rooms, but it was not and could never be a home. Before her on the table was a pot of tea, but it was stewed now.

As soon as Gerry arrived, Izzy rushed to embrace her. The force of her gladness and relief surprised both of them. 'Thank goodness you're all right!'

'Of course I'm all right. What's got into you?' Detaching herself from her daughter, Gerry left the room before Izzy could reply and headed upstairs. Izzy was a queer one, she could tell when something was up. Was she having one of her turns? Gerry didn't want her asking any questions, so she fired a few at her on her way out: 'Is Annie still off on Bramble? And did you give the Bairn his two o'clock? I should have asked your dad to get some more milk . . .'. But no sooner had she left than she was hurrying back downstairs, all need-to-know: 'Where is he? Your brother. Where's Raymond?'

Izzy was pouring the tea down the sink. Once that was done, and it had all gone away down the pipes to be swallowed at a future date by the North Sea, she turned to look at her mam, standing in the door.

'Where is he? Where's your brother?' Gerry said again.

It was a new thing, this, hearing a true note of panic in her mother's voice. It made Izzy realise how much she had grown used to hearing the note of pretend-panic. 'Isn't he in his cot?' she asked.

'No, he isn't. Of course he isn't. I wouldn't be asking you if he was there, you little idiot!'

Mam was getting angry now. That was disappointing, but Izzy supposed she should have expected it, and anyway, she felt, for maybe the first time ever, at a terrific remove from her mother's anger, which was like an explosion on the seabed, while Izzy sat safe in her little boat, a mile above it all, bobbing.

'Maybe Dad's got him . . .' she said. 'Where *is* Dad, by the way?'

'He's not with your dad. Your dad's in Eshwood, running some errand. He didn't take the Bairn with him. I asked him to, but he wouldn't. He wouldn't. He wouldn't take him and give me an afternoon off. Jesus Christ. Jesus Christ. Where is he?'

7

Four hours later all the men of Eshwood, or so it seemed, were out with sticks and dogs. They were holding formation, three feet apart, advancing through the woods. All were silent, for it was getting dark now, and no one wanted to admit it, or talk about what it might mean if they didn't find the Bairn soon. Only the soft crash of a stick through the undergrowth, an occasional grunted instruction to a dog, the choked bluster of a startled pheasant.

Annie had never seen their rooms in Eshwood Hall so packed full of people. She stood and watched and wondered. She knew that she should keep quiet above all. Two policemen were there. One was writing things down and looking up now and then at the other one who wasn't doing anything. Sheila was there and Sheila's husband Bob was there and their daughter Biddy was there and Mr Henderson the gamekeeper was there and other people who worked at the Hall whose names she couldn't remember were there too. Mr Henderson was wearing his woolly socks and funny trousers called plus fours. Dad was home now and he kept looking around the room like he didn't know what was going on.

Annie should have been in bed by now but something was happening. Mam had obviously been crying because her eyes were puffy and she looked like she was going to start again, except she kept making herself cough and the coughing seemed to stop the crying. The first policeman had closed his notebook and stood up now. Dad was trying to put his arm around Mam but she didn't want him to. Mr Henderson was organising the men into another search party and telling them which bit of the forest to make a start with. There were so many people here, but the Bairn wasn't here, and Annie kept wondering, where's the Bairn? which was silly because nobody knew where the Bairn was, and that's why everyone was here. Annie looked over at Izzy, but Izzy was ignoring her like always.

Izzy was keeping quiet as well, but, as she was older than Annie, she was used to keeping quiet while the grown-ups were talking. Everyone was murmuring, filling the room with a breathless flow of sound. It occurred to Izzy that she was seeing something that she had seen many times before: a room full of men arranged around the figure of her mam, circling her in a slow, awkward dance that none of them would have actually admitted was a dance. They were drones gathered around a queen, buzz-buzz, eager to perform whatever ministries were required. It was something she had seen before, yes, but this time, of course, her mam wasn't laughing, as she usually was.

Then Gerry caught Izzy looking, and her mouth changed, as something took shape within her. Izzy watched her mother. She saw her mother's eyes, how they seemed to sharpen each time she blinked. She blinked three times. It was as though the scene were hanging suspended in egg white.

When Gerry spoke, her voice seemed thick and far away at first: 'You. *You!* Where is he? Just . . . *sitting* there . . . What have you done with him?' Gerry was on her feet now. All eyes were on her.

'I haven't done anything with anyone!' Izzy was back in the beating present moment now, retreating before Gerry.

Gerry sprang at her, grabbed her and shook her in a frenzy: '*Where is he? Where is he?*' She was screaming now, and when Izzy didn't reply – after Ray and the policeman had drawn Gerry, as gently as they could manage, away from her daughter and she had ceased to struggle against them – she, Gerry, asked her daughter, in the ensuing silence and with a terrible conviction, where she had been that afternoon.

There are occasions, though mercifully few, when our eyes give up our entire selves; anyone who then met our gaze with an open heart would see us – like a dweller standing at the threshold of two little windows – in the raw. This moment chanced to be one such for both Izzy and Gerry. In those seconds they apprehended each other truly for the first time, and Gerry, though her face drained of blood, did not look away when Izzy replied, 'I was helping Hobbs. I was helping the gardener. Where were you?'

*

At last light they found him, they found the Bairn, Raymond. Into his mouth and his nose had been stuffed handfuls of grass and mud. Daisies laid on his eyes. Later, the men wouldn't remember which of them had found the little blue-veined body, whose cry had rung out, whose dog had howled. As they'd never speak of it again, they'd never know for sure. But they knew who carried him back to the Hall, for it was agreed that that should be the priest, Father Lawrence, who was at hand, helping in the search, and so that's what happened. They'd never look at him quite the same way after that. Already a silence was beginning, reaching over everyone present and closing its grip; a silence that would last as long as they lasted, and that they would guard should any stranger come foolish enough to threaten it; and even years later, if one of their boys – in the Garland, in a lull after the older men have been talking of something – ever asks about that day, he'll get a cuff round the ear and a promise of more later.

*

The year had begun to die, and soon the Whippers' Humber Hawk would be making its way down the driveway from Eshwood Hall for the last time, its headlights pushing back the darkness like a plough, chasing the shadows back into the trees. First, the Whippers would once more have to carry boxes and drag bags into the car. Picture them: Ray carrying armfuls of bedding downstairs, and Gerry taking her collection of china figurines from the Welsh dresser, gazing dumbfounded at them and at whoever had collected them in the first place. One by one into the box go the dolls, not to come out again.

Bramble will not accompany the family when they leave. Annie, who was moving on from her horse craze, took the news better than Ray could have hoped for, and with her father she ceremoniously set Bramble free the morning of their departure. Alas, it seemed the animal, who would not in any case survive the winter, disrelished his first taste of freedom, and meekly took himself into the stable block, to wait there for whatever was going to happen next.

Ray's crate of circuit boards, transistors, bulbs, batteries and condensers will also stay at the Hall. Ray will simply forget to pack them. The decision to leave them behind is a good one, even if, like all of his choices, Ray hadn't been aware of making it.

Like a good girl, Annie has gathered the Bairn's toys together – objects once; emblems now – and after she has packed them away she starts carefully wrapping crockery in newspaper. From across the room, her sister watches her. Always a quiet one, Izzy talks less and less these days. She rarely has occasion to speak. Another kind of silence, that of a deep well, has opened before her, and she may perhaps topple in – for a time. But for now she is happy to sit, a hand under her head, watching her sister work.

Outside, all across Eshwood Forest, horse-chestnut leaves are crimsoning, the larches blaze their yellows, and holly berries redden. The short hours will shorten, and the fogs and the mists and the battering rains foretell the winter that is on its way.

Epilogue

from the case notes of
Dr Erasmus Wintergreen

Friday 13 June 1919

[. . .] I continue to be fascinated by the case of Private M, who, although showing signs of recovery in other aspects, remains in the grip of a delusion that there is a man living in the forest here at Eshwood: a man, indeed, not just living in the trees, but composed and constituted of them, and able to appear from – and disappear into – them at will. This delusion is remarkable in that there were no signs of it prior to M's arrival at the clinic.

Apart from this, and the fact that he is a private rather than an officer, his case history is typical. Upon arrival, he exhibited what may be considered the classic symptoms of war neurosis: chronic insomnia, refusing food, and elective muteness (though I do the term 'elective' a certain amount of violence in saying so). An especially long and taxing session of hypnotherapy coaxed him back into speech, and when it did, he at once commenced to tell anyone who would listen all about this wild man in the woods he'd been seeing. Not that these encounters trouble him: he speaks with a kind of pity for us that we have not met with the fellow ourselves.

Whether this imaginary companion will prove to be a spirit of consolation (the embodiment, as it were, of M's fallen comrades) or a vengeful scourge (the embodiment, as it were, of the men M has slain) remains to be seen. In either case I am inclined to see him as a healthful figure, the product of a psyche that has been placed under much too severe a strain, certainly, but a psyche that is also fighting back, albeit with phantasmagorical fire of its own. M is undergoing a great change, and even if it transpires that this change is in the immediate future a breakdown, it will be one that precipitates his return to the world.

Of this I am certain: to hear M tell of his encounters with this fellow, you would be hard pressed to remain on the better side of half-believing him. Perhaps that is what leads me to say this for posterity: if M is correct, and it is no delusion, then I may be about to discover a new species. I shall call him *Homo nemorensis* – 'the man of the grove' – very good!